**"I WON'T HAVE YOU TREATING ME LIKE
. . . A GROUPIE, NO MATTER HOW GREAT A
HOCKEY STAR YOU THINK YOU ARE!"**

"I'm sorry, but we're adults, Elaine, and everyone
knows we've been together. There's no sense in trying to hide it. You've got to start acting your age."

"That's just it, Roland. I am acting my age. I'm a
woman of thirty-two who enjoys her privacy. And
I'm a woman who doesn't like being manhandled in
front of some lecherous hockey player."

"Is that really it? Is it just your privacy you're worried about, or have you suddenly gotten cold feet?
Don't forget, I didn't exactly force you to make love
with me. We *both* wanted it. Or do you always tire so
easily of a man?"

# CANDLELIGHT ECSTASY ROMANCES®

# CALLING THE SHOTS

*Kathy Alerding*

*A CANDLELIGHT ECSTASY ROMANCE®*

Published by
Dell Publishing Co., Inc.
1 Dag Hammarskjold Plaza
New York, New York 10017

Dell ® TM 681510, Dell Publishing Co., Inc.

Candlelight Ecstasy Romance®, 1,203,540, is a registered
trademark of Dell Publishing Co., Inc., New York, New York.

ISBN: 0-440-11054-8

Printed in the United States of America

First printing—August 1985

To Our Readers:

We have been delighted with your enthusiastic response to Candlelight Ecstasy Romances®, and we thank you for the interest you have shown in this exciting series.

In the upcoming months we will continue to present the distinctive sensuous love stories you have come to expect only from Ecstasy. We look forward to bringing you many more books from your favorite authors and also the very finest work from new authors of contemporary romantic fiction.

As always, we are striving to present the unique, absorbing love stories that you enjoy most—books that are more than ordinary romance. Your suggestions and comments are always welcome. Please write to us at the address below.

Sincerely,

The Editors
Candlelight Romances
1 Dag Hammarskjold Plaza
New York, New York 10017

# CHAPTER ONE

Soft, rhythmic sounds filled the crisp, cold air around her: the low drone of steel over ice; the muted tapping of wood on the frozen surface of the arena. She closed her eyes so that no other sensation could distract her from the familiar sounds that greeted her that early-fall morning.

Still bent over her skates, she sat motionless, relaxed—hands frozen in mid-action of threading the long laces through leather eyelets—and just listened.

The air was crystal clear and cold as it moved across the rink and swirled around the wooden bench where she sat. Its clean, sharp feel added to the pleasure of the moment by mixing sound and scent with fond memories of seasons past and the anticipation of a new one just beginning.

For a brief moment Elaine became part of the atmosphere, more than a physical participant on the scene. Her heart seemed to beat with the same rhythm made by the few idle skaters who skimmed, voiceless, over the ice before her. Eyes still closed, she sensed the blood rushing through her veins with increasing force. She felt like a long-absent child returning home. Memories triggered by the icy sounds around her began to flood her with pleasant anticipation.

Elaine was home there where she belonged, where she had always belonged. A well of warm tears mounted slowly in her eyes. They were tears of reunion and homecoming, but she allowed them only a temporary stay before opening her eyes once more and brushing them quickly away.

She had no time for sentimentality. There was work to be done. Another season of her life was about to begin.

"Hey, Doc!" A voice broke through her trance, and Elaine looked up to see the familiar face of Pete Hadly whisking past her. "Better hurry up, you're late," he shouted over his shoulder.

"No, I'm not," she shouted in return, smiling. "You're early!"

She quickly secured the laces of her skates and stood to walk across a rubber mat leading to the rink. As she glided out onto the ice, twelve eager bodies dressed in matching red and white practice uniforms bounded onto the ice opposite her, and the shimmering air suddenly crackled with laughter and yelps of total, unbridled enthusiasm.

As she took her warm-up laps, Elaine carefully sized up the new recruits, while she looked for the six players who had been held over from the previous season. Within a few laps she'd welcomed back the old-timers and at least shaken hands with all the new players.

"Hi, Doc, 'member me?" one young man asked.

"Sure, I do. It's Rutledge. How's your ankle?"

"Lots better. Did all those exercises you suggested over the summer, and it's feelin' fine," the husky redhead answered readily.

"Good. But I want to check you out after practice. My office at four, okay?" She struck his shoulder lightly as he passed, grinning at her.

As always, Elaine remembered each man by name, uniform number, and previous injuries. It had become a ritual at the beginning of each season for her to renew old ties by asking about each player's progress over the summer and making initial appointments for follow-ups during the first practice morning.

Not only did her memory and interest seem to please the

players, but it served to spark her back into the routine after the five-month break. She was no longer on vacation; she was a trainer again. And experience had shown her that the quicker she and the team got back into the swing of serious hockey, the better.

They had been in warm-up for nearly half an hour when she noticed Cap Holloway's arrival. At sixty-seven he was an impressive sight. With a full crown of snow-white hair framing his broad, ruddy face, the older man she'd come to know and admire looked more like a kindly grandfather than the dynamic, demanding coach he was.

"Okay, men. Listen up," Holloway bellowed above the din of chatter. Immediately the unorganized crowd of young men moved to center ice to face their coach in respectful silence.

"All of you have already met me, so there's not much need to run over that old ground again. You know what I want, and you know what I expect of each of you. Though I've worked with only a few of you before, I have no doubts about the capabilities you new men possess. And after we've been together for a while, you'll see that I won't accept less than your best."

While the coach produced his cut-and-dried preseason speech, Elaine, who stood at the edge of the players' cluster, took a long look at the team she would be working with this year. She paid particularly close attention to the new men, whom she'd have to get to know very well in a very short time.

All were sturdily built, and most stood between five feet eight inches and six feet, except for one player, who towered over the others at six feet four inches. His height could be a serious disadvantage, she thought. In hockey, speed and agility were essential. A taller player was prone to serious injury because his height offset the natural balance required on skates. She made a mental note to work with him on building graceful control.

All in all, the rest of the new recruits were very typical of those she had worked with over the past eight years. Enthusiastic, muscular, and energetic—and at least twelve years younger than she—they looked healthy and self-assured. But as always, they would need discipline and work if they wanted to move into the majors. Each had potential, but from experience, she knew that only a few would have that important combination of drive and determination to turn their talent into a dream career of major-league hockey.

"And now that you've met the coaching staff, I want to introduce you to our senior trainer, Elaine D'Arte," she heard the coach finally say.

As usual, she took his cue and skated to the front of the group. And as usual, her introduction was greeted with whistles and players' nudging each other in silent comment. Elaine had come to take their unorthodox compliments in stride. She neither smiled nor acknowledged the ruckus but ignored it until Coach Holloway had finished his part of their thoroughly rehearsed performance.

"Well," the coach continued, after the clamor died down, "I guess we won't have to go through eye exams this season. It's obvious you guys have twenty/twenty."

His comments drew appropriate laughter, yet Elaine stood still without giving a clue to her reaction to it all.

"And I'm glad to see you're all healthy, red-blooded specimens who can appreciate a nice-looking woman," continued Holloway. "But let's get it straight from the beginning. It's Miss D'Arte or Doc, if you like, and no exceptions. We're proud to have one of the finest trainers in hockey working with this team, and you're to give her every respect. Got that?"

His undiluted statement sobered the players immediately, and several even nodded in affirmation.

"Good. Now, every practice session will start with a full hour on the ice with Miss D'Arte. She will work with you on

12

speed, stamina, agility. The assistant coaches will then take over with standard drills for another hour, and our last hour on the ice each morning will be spent developing plays."

A furtive groan rose like a soft hum among the players, but Holloway ignored it.

"That's the morning schedule for weekdays. In addition, I expect each of you to complete three hours each afternoon at the gym. Phil Walters will monitor your gym time, and in conjunction with your trainer's recommendations, he'll create individual body-building programs for each of you. Any questions?"

Surprisingly their communal groaning over the rigorous, preseason schedule was not evident in their questions. As with the start of every new season, the players' primary questions revolved around equipment needs, lost luggage, and housing problems, all of which Holloway took in stride and assigned to one of the assistant coaches for processing and solving.

"All right, if there aren't any more questions, I'll leave you to get started with your trainer. And, men"—Holloway lowered his bull-like voice and looked directly into the faces of the new team members—"remember, we're all here to build a winning team. You have your jobs, and the coaching staff has theirs. But the Hawks are a team. A family of sorts. If you need help, you need to talk out a problem—whether it's hockey or personal—we want to help you. Don't hesitate to ask. Part of being a winner in this world is knowing when you need help and having the guts to ask for it. Understood?"

Each player silently nodded. A few older players even smiled, knowing that Holloway faithfully stood by his words.

"Okay then. Let's get down to it. We want a winning season!"

A roar of acknowledgment went up as Holloway skated

off the ice, accompanied by the remainder of the staff. Only Elaine was left to start the workout.

"I want to welcome the new players, and I'm glad to see so few regulars around this season," she said, and her comments were greeted with laughter. In her own way she had complimented the returning players. It was public knowledge that nearly half the previous season's team had been called up to the parent club, an outstanding record for any minor-league team.

"Although I haven't gotten to know any of you rookies yet, in the next four weeks we'll get better acquainted." Someone made a sly comment, and Elaine caught a glimpse of one player elbowing another into silence.

"Now, I want to start you out on a primary obstacle course," she said authoritatively. "If you're going to be outstanding hockey players, you must develop keen agility, along with speed. So spread out," she commanded, "and let's get going."

Reluctantly the team followed her to one end of the rink, where a complex array of pylons and low hurdles stood.

"It's essential that you all master this obstacle maze. How well you maneuver and control your skates will determine how well you take hard body contact in play," she explained to them. Body checks—intense body contact— were the most damaging encounters faced by a hockey player. Being able to avoid high-speed impact was of top priority in avoiding serious injury.

Elaine pointed out the course structure as she continued with detailed instructions. "We'll take the course over and over with increased speed, but I want you to follow me through the first time slowly. When you understand what's expected, I'll let you go on your own at a faster pace."

Elaine skated to the first obstacle: two folding chairs, set facing each other. "I want you to do a forward tumble over the chair seats and land on both skates," she said to the group and then immediately tumbled over the chairs and

14

landed squarely on both feet. "But meet each obstacle in motion," she went on, skating back toward the chairs, "like this!" Without slowing down, Elaine again approached the chairs, put her head down to her chest, folded her arms into her midsection, pulled her knees in under her chin, and, curled up in a tight ball, somersaulted over the chairs and faced the group again.

They all continued through the course, with Elaine explaining and demonstrating the way through the labyrinth of barriers. There were low hurdles for jumping and arrangements of pylons for tight circling. Some pylons were color-coded—a signal for the players to reverse and skate backward to the next obstacle. It was a complicated maneuvering course, designed to challenge even the most nimble, experienced skater.

After a single run-through Elaine released the players, in single file, to get the feel of the course. The first two runs through the maze went fairly well because Elaine kept the pace slow and even.

The players, though grumbling or laughing to cover their personal uncertainties, appeared to have smooth, well-balanced skills at the slower pace.

Elaine increased their tempo on the third round and had the team skating at much greater speed through the course. The men looked fairly good, even though she noticed that a few players were beginning to experience coordination problems. Those were the ones she would have to give extra attention to.

The fourth round required maximum skill; the team was moving at near game-level speed. This time two players went down on the ice almost immediately, unable to coordinate their movements effectively. To minimize embarrassment, Elaine never changed her manner or voice, even though she was concerned that they might be hurt.

"Pick yourselves up," she called and was relieved to see

both young men scramble to their feet. "You two get the silver helmet award for the day."

There was mixed laughter and gibing, and both players' faces turned bright red.

"Watching this group work out reminds me of roller derby tryouts," she said jokingly. "Any one of you would be just right for a remake of the *Kansas City Bombers!*"

As she hoped, the humor repaired any ego damage. By referring to the entire group, she'd lessened the embarrassment for the two who'd fallen.

The hour was finished, much to the delight of the players, who cheered at the announcement.

"Okay, that's it for today! We'll keep this course pattern up for the balance of the week, and then next Monday we'll see what you can really do."

She turned and skated off the ice, to be greeted by Phil Walters, an assistant coach.

"How do they look?" he asked.

"Not bad," Elaine replied. "We have about five who are going to need some work, but all in all, it looks like a fair season ahead. What do you think?"

"I think you haven't seen it all yet" was his peculiar reply. "Holloway wants you in his office right away. He's got a big surprise for you."

"Oh? Am I going to like it?" she asked her friend.

"I don't know," Phil said with a grin. "I just met him, and I'm not sure what to think yet. But I guarantee you that this is going to be an interesting season at the very least." With that he skated onto the ice, and Elaine sat down, puzzled, to remove her skates.

---

Cap Holloway's office was an odd combination of memorabilia, stacks of team photographs, mountains of incomplete paper work and dust. Yet it had a touch of sophistication and genuine accomplishment. The older man's life was reflected on the walls in awards and souvenir photos;

his greatest pride, however, was evidenced by almost a dozen league trophies—the only items in the office that were regularly polished and pampered.

Though his door was seldom closed, Elaine arrived to find the office secured. She knocked, and when she was told to enter, a custom not often required, she suddenly felt uncomfortable about her "surprise."

"Did you want to see me, Cap?" she asked, entering the office cautiously.

"I sure did, Elaine. Is your session finished?" He didn't wait for a reply. Instead, he stood and nodded toward the corner. "I want you to meet the newest member of the Omaha Hawks."

Elaine had to close the door to see the corner Holloway had indicated. Amazed, she found herself staring at Roland Pantier.

Although they had never met before, she recognized him immediately. The soft black hair and intense raven eyes were familiar to hockey professionals and fans throughout the Americas. Although she'd seen his picture many times, had watched him play on cable, Elaine was stunned to find him even more devastatingly alluring than she had expected.

His professional nickname was the Panther, coined to describe his quick, catlike movements on skates. But his deep black eyes and beguiling grin, the powerful, muscular curves of his compact six-foot-tall body indicated to Elaine that even off the ice this man could be overpowering.

Trying to remain calm and composed, she held out her hand when he stood to greet her. They exchanged a quick handshake, but Elaine found the sensation of his warm, hard hand distressing. For some reason, Elaine felt suddenly off-balance and terribly shaken.

*How ridiculous,* she thought. *I've met hundreds of pros better-looking than he.* The small lie seemed to ease her back to reality.

"Miss D'Arte," he said. His voice was like dark silk, with a Quebec accent. "My pleasure." Their handshake was finished, but he held on to her hand and let his gaze roam across her face with disconcerting curiosity.

"Pantier, isn't it?" she said, trying to conceal how deeply he had affected her.

"Roland, please. Everyone calls me Roland," he said.

Elaine knew she had given him the wrong signal. Her surprise at seeing him in Holloway's office had obviously been misinterpreted as the standard reaction. She must look like a star-struck hockey fan, and he was eating it up, she thought with a tinge of anger.

Pulling her hand out of his, Elaine straightened and sent a more appropriate signal back to him. "I think Mr. Pantier would be a better choice." She smiled wryly. "After all, we've just met."

"Ah, not so, really," he answered in a flash. "I've heard about you for a long time. You have quite a reputation as a trainer, you know. And it's obvious you know me if only by reputation also, but then we are colleagues, yes? Both professionals in the same field?"

"Of course you are!" interjected Holloway, who had not caught the nuance of their conversation. "Let's turn off the formality here. It's Elaine, Roland." Holloway caught himself. "But I prefer, for professional reasons, that all players refer to Elaine as Miss D'Arte or Doc, if you like," he went on.

"Then I will abide by that, of course. Still, your name is so descriptive, Miss D'Arte. Elaine, an object of art."

Elaine had grown very annoyed with Pantier's smooth jock performance. "So, you speak Italian, Mr. Pantier?" she said, referring to the fact that he had recognized the meaning of her last name.

"No, not really. But there's not so much difference between French and Italian—at least not much between certain words. Your name is easy—"

18

"Only the name," she interrupted, to ensure that her point would not be missed.

Both Pantier and Holloway caught her meaning, and the coach decided to take the initiative before this meeting dissolved in a battle of wills.

"Take a seat, Elaine," he said casually, and she moved to the only other available chair in the office—the one next to Pantier, who, unruffled by her comment, sat down placidly next to her.

"I'm sure you're familiar with Roland's outstanding career with Edmonton, Elaine," the coach said. He smiled and nodded at Pantier, whose grin broadened at Holloway's acknowledgment. "And it's because of his illustrious career that the team owners have decided to use him as a minor-league scout for the first half of this season."

"A few weeks at the very most," Pantier interjected firmly but still smilingly. "I've been instructed to scout opposing teams in early-season play to see if there's any raw talent out there that Edmonton could use."

In other words, Elaine thought, Pantier was to watch for new players who could be persuaded to join the organization the next season. It made sense, but something about Pantier's insisting that his scouting assignment was for just "a few weeks" didn't ring right to her.

"So you think you'll need only a month or so to accomplish your mission?" she questioned. "I thought scouting involved at least a full season of observation and evaluation."

Pantier remained undisturbed by her logical, precise comment. "Perhaps, to a less experienced eye," he replied. "For me, a month at most will give me all I need to know."

Elaine was about to remind him that it would be at least two months before the Hawks completed a single round of competition with all the other clubs in the league when Holloway reentered the conversation.

"Roland's assignment with the Hawks is open-ended

right now. How long he's with us will be determined by the big brass at Edmonton. Meanwhile," he went on, "let's get him signed on. Regular procedures and all. For starters, I want you, Elaine, to arrange for a routine team physical and evaluation for Roland this afternoon."

"I doubt a physical is necessary," Pantier said. "I'm in top condition." He gave Elaine a slow wink.

"I think I'll be the judge of that," she said in quick rebuttal.

"Yes, Elaine's the boss in this area, and what she says goes around here—at least when it comes to player evaluation," Holloway said stoutly.

"Then you're a physician?" Pantier asked with a broad grin, knowing that she was not an M.D.

"No, I'm certified in sports medicine and physical therapy," she replied.

"And yet they call you Doc?" Pantier said, his thick, trimmed brows arching at her playfully. Elaine ruffled, but before she could speak, Holloway stepped in again.

"It's a compliment the team designated to her years ago," said Holloway, who had finally caught the complete drift of the three-way conversation. He decided to work around Pantier's ego as diplomatically as possible. "In all the years I've worked with Miss D'Arte, I've never known our team physician to disagree with her examination procedures, diagnoses, or therapy programs."

"That's quite an impressive record," Pantier commented.

"Yes, it is. I suggest you get settled in here, stow your gear, and make an appointment with Miss D'Arte to go over your medical records and have a look at you. It's standard procedure for everyone—players and staff." Holloway stood behind the desk and missed the brash, inviting look which the hockey player flashed at Elaine and which she ignored.

"Tomorrow afternoon, after practice, we'll send you

over for a review with Dr. Morton, our team's M.D. Until then," Holloway said, exending his hand to Pantier but now less cordially than before.

Pantier took the hint that the meeting was over and stood to shake the coach's hand. He turned back to Elaine, holding out his hand again.

"It's been my pleasure," he said, smiling, but she did not offer a farewell handshake. "I'm looking forward to working with you." Unbothered by her silence, Pantier smiled again, picked up his gym bag, and left the office, closing the door behind him.

Elaine was still shaken by the incident. She realized how poorly she'd managed her surprise and the fascinating yet overpowering impact Pantier had had on her.

"We've got a tough one to deal with here," said Holloway, who apparently had not noticed Elaine's physical response to Pantier.

Taking a deep breath, Elaine tried to produce a calm, neutral effect, but her pulse still raced. Pantier's image seemed etched in her mind's eye. She shook herself mentally, concentrated on Holloway's words, and tried to think of her job.

"I remember he was injured during that game last season, but I thought the surgery turned out quite well," she commented.

"Oh, it did. That's not it, Elaine. It's his age." Holloway just shook his head. "Pantier's been worth his weight in gold to the Oilers. Just having his name on the player roster for a game intimidated the competition." Holloway returned to the swivel chair behind his desk. "No, the team owners are convinced his playing days are coming to an end. It's too bad. He's got three years left on his contract, and they want to squeeze it for everything he's worth until they retire him. That's why he's here."

Elaine could fill in the rest. It was the oldest demon known to plague athletes—age. Pantier was thirty-eight, and though in good physical condition generally, he was pushing the outermost limits for a hockey player.

Edmonton's owners had signed a number of outstanding rookies for the coming season and were hoping Pantier would not really be needed. Putting him out to scout was the first sign that the owners were ready to work him out of the pros.

"Will he get to play for Edmonton at all this season?" Elaine asked Cap. Arrogant as Pantier might have been, she felt a sincere pang of remorse for his situation. Of course, he wanted to be back and playing in a few weeks; possibly he would not let himself believe that his professional playing days were nearly over.

"It's hard to say," replied the coach with a heavy sigh. "If they need him badly enough, of course, they'll call him back. But Edmonton looks awfully strong right now." Holloway shook his head soberly.

"What do you want me to do?" she asked.

"Well, it's a job for all of us, as usual. I personally want to make his assignment here pleasant for all concerned. But I want you to start with the regular routine tests and checks, so we know just where he is physically. As far as I can tell, from talking it over with the owners, they don't want him playing here as such. He's with the Hawks for scouting— remember that. But we also want him to stay in shape just in case he's called back to Edmonton during the season."

"That's going to make it tougher, Cap. It doesn't take an expert to see that the guy's gung ho on playing."

"I know. And if he shows an interest in playing with the Hawks, I'll give him a go once in a while. But in my estimation, Pantier's still too valuable a player to risk in minor-league play." Unwrapping a thick cigar, Holloway sighed again and leaned back in his chair. "We'll just have to play it by ear, Elaine. I'd hate to be the guy to tell Pantier—"

He stopped in mid-sentence, but Elaine knew what he was thinking. Roland Pantier's career was at stake, and no one would want to theorize on his future. She had been associated with sports nearly all her life, and Elaine D'Arte knew—better than most—how devastating it was to hear that a competitive athletic career was finished.

"I'll do what I can, Cap," she said, standing to leave.

"Just take that French macho stuff for what it's worth," he counseled. "But if he really gets out of line, let me know. Okay?"

"Sure" was all she could say. She couldn't understand why she felt oddly depressed. After all, she hardly knew Pantier.

## CHAPTER TWO

That first morning passed quickly, with players arriving at Elaine's office for routine exams and evaluations of past-season injuries.

The concentration required helped her push any thought of Roland Pantier into the farther recesses of her conscious mind. His image and the memory of the high-voltage quality of their initial meeting were subdued as she worked on the concerns of her daily clinical barrage of therapy, questions, and suggestions.

Lunch hour came and went, but Elaine remained in her office—too busy, she thought, to be bothered with food. Yet she realized that it was just a means of avoiding Pantier. She would have to adjust to him and the unusual attraction she felt for him eventually, but for now she had forestalled another encounter.

Late that afternoon, as she sat, trying to submerge herself in a set of X rays, Elaine sensed a chill ripple down her spine. She knew that someone was behind her. Slowly she turned to face the door, and there, as she had suspected, stood Roland Pantier.

Dressed in a practice uniform, still carrying his helmet and hockey stick, he seemed more impressive than ever. Hair, damp and tousled, clung to his head, and wisps of black curls rose about his ears. He smiled that playful grin she'd seen in Holloway's office, his eyes sparkling enticingly from beneath dense dark brows.

Elaine took a long, purposeful breath as she turned back to the file on her desk. "You can drop your gear over there," she said, pointing to a small table but not looking directly at him. "Then get up on the examining table."

Again she just pointed, making sure not to look into his eyes, wanting a moment to compose herself. She occupied herself by shuffling through the small mountain of medical reports and file folders on her desk and kept her back to him.

"Should I undress?" he finally asked.

"That won't be necessary," Elaine replied in a monotone as her heart tried to abandon her body in one gigantic thud.

"Not even just a little?" She heard his question but ignored it.

With some effort Elaine finally located his medical history file and opened it as she approached the examining table in her best professional posture. Without looking up or speaking, she took several minutes to digest its contents and even punctuated her silence with a few very professional sighs and hm's.

"How do you feel?" she asked, still not looking away from the file.

Pantier thoughtfully patted his body from his chest down to his thigh. "About the same as I did this morning." He grinned as he replied. "Would you like a report on how I feel later?"

"I meant—" She looked at him sharply.

"Oh," he said quickly, "I'm a little stiff at times. But I'm in excellent condition otherwise."

"Were you told that by a doctor, or is that your own diagnosis?" Fortunately Elaine's voice did not betray the unbalanced sensation that again rose to claim her. Her voice was calm, professional, and tinged with an unimpressed, almost uninterested quality, and she allowed it to camouflage her natural response to his humor. A strong,

25

disturbing flutter of excitement kept trying to envelop her, and she fought it down.

"I don't need a doctor to tell me what's normal within my own body," Pantier said to her. "After all, I've lived within this frame for a lifetime. I know it well. I'm a little stiff from time to time, and that's to be expected after a long hockey career." His words were harsh, but the tone of his voice remained smooth and undaunted.

Elaine's eyes shot from the file and met his directly. She had understood the undercurrent of rebuke in his statement, and was determined to set their relationship straight. She would not have a player diagnosing his own physical status.

"That's all very interesting, Mr. Pantier," she replied flatly, "but within your own statement I find a flaw in your reasoning."

"And how is that, Miss Work of Art?" His question dripped with contempt, but Elaine was able to control her gaze and her tone.

"You have suffered many injuries in the course of your career—"

"Of course," he interrupted coolly. "Occupational hazard."

"Yes, an occupational hazard that becomes more difficult to deal with after each additional injury. What I see in your X rays indicates that you are as reckless a player as I've ever seen. At your age—"

The cold, undiplomatic sound of her own words nearly made Elaine cringe. In her defensiveness she had carelessly lashed out in a manner she could not easily condone.

Still, holding Pantier's eyes with her own, she searched his expression to find a clue to how he had taken her heartless statement. Black as night and just as mysterious, his eyes were unchanged.

It was Elaine who broke eye contact to return to the

medical file. She remained silent, trying to calm the pounding in her head and the trembling in her limbs.

"I have scars, yes," Pantier said slowly at last. "You give very little credit to the body's ability to heal itself and return to normal functioning," he added, watching her.

"I credit all healing to the body's own natural ability," Elaine replied matter-of-factly.

"Then we have no quarrel, Miss D'Arte." His voice was clear, and his manner determined. Yet Elaine recognized the stoic signs of his inability to acknowledge the truth. With more diplomacy and a subtle change of tone, she began again.

"Let's take a look at you and see where we are," she said as she put the file aside and motioned for him to recline on the padded table.

"Ah, now I undress." He chuckled, still staring at her.

"I think that will be quite unnecessary," she replied, pointing to the knee-length shorts he had on. "I'll just remove your knee and shin guards." She moved to the table, where he reclined without comment, smiling roguishly.

Although she *had* to touch Pantier to examine him properly, a sudden panic gripped Elaine as she reached out to the exquisitely fashioned body before her. She stripped away the guards, and with hands nearly trembling, Elaine moved along the finely defined muscles of his lower thigh. With gentle cupped hands, she traced around one knee and slowly down onto his calf, following the natural flow of muscles and tendons.

His well-developed legs were thickly banded in broad, tanned muscle and covered with fine black hair that moved like down beneath her touch. Even though she tried to concentrate solely on the primary reason for the examination, Elaine's mind raced, and her imagination began to fashion an image of the rest of his body: an image drawn from the exciting sensations she received as her palms ran slowly over the length of his lower extremities.

"You have a healing touch," Pantier murmured alluringly. His voice drew Elaine back from the realm of imagination with a jolt.

He lay there on his back with arms crossed beneath his head, smiling with unabashed pleasure, and she wondered if the heat within her was so obvious.

She realized that it was when he said, "Why do you blush, Miss D'Arte?" His teasing tone and the now obvious physical response her hands had evoked in his body brought Elaine back to reality. A jolt of anger—anger at her own fascination—reduced her pulsing excitement, and she lifted her hands slowly from his leg.

She tried to reach for the medical file again, a fairly safe retreat from the reality of the situation, but as she moved away from the table, Pantier's hand quickly slid up her arm to hold her in place.

Speechless, as his touch sent additional voltage into her body, she met his gaze and stood trembling beside him.

"Why do you deny our mutual attraction?" he asked softly, his dark eyes snapping with fire. "You are a beautiful woman who must be used to her effect on men. Yet you seem so"—he thought for a split second and smiled as he added—"inexperienced."

The interlude gave Elaine just enough time to recover some measure of composure, and his statement provided just the right elements for a cutting reply.

"I've had plenty of experience," she snapped. "I've been in this business long enough to recognize a jock who gets his kicks from charming and seducing star-struck women." With a jerk she pulled free of his grasp. "So you can cut the act. I'm not interested."

His eyes narrowed slightly, but the smile remained. "You're not?" he questioned boldly.

"Not hardly," she replied with renewed anger. "It's time you realize that this is a professional relationship!"

As she retrieved his file, Elaine felt a new form of anger

flood full force to the surface of her mind. Turning to face the examining table, she listened—almost passively—as her words fell, knife-edged, into the room.

"I've really had it with all this macho jock garbage, Pantier. I don't stand for it with the rookies, and I won't stand for it with you. Superstar status is null and void with me." Although her voice was steady, her legs shook noticeably.

The room was silent. The examination continued routinely, and when it was over, Elaine returned to his file and began making notations. Thankful for the anger that had materialized to rescue her, she now tried to put it aside, and reclaim the more compassionate side of her nature.

Elaine had made her point, and Pantier seemed to accept it.

"Do you have any questions?" she asked after detailing her notes in his chart.

"Not that I can think of," he replied, swinging his legs over the edge of the table and stepping to the floor. His tamer manner, after their brief confrontation, was all she required to put them back on a more positive footing.

"Ah, yes, there is one question." Pantier's eyes sparkled as he picked up his gear and started for the door. Turning back toward Elaine with a broad grin, he asked, "Is there any time you ask a player to get undressed in here?"

"Only for certain injuries," she replied, idly looking at his file.

"Then I'll try to injure my 'certain' next time," he said, opening the door.

"Out!" she shouted as he closed the door, and then she sat down hard at the desk, not knowing whether to laugh or to throw something at the door.

Try as she might to concentrate on other things, the remainder of the day was lost in personal thoughts: about Pantier, her unpredictable responses to him, and the continuing tingle of excitement, mixed with a rare kind of anger, that dominated their interaction.

She'd met his type before but had never experienced such a pronounced physical reaction. Usually one direct refusal had been enough to deflect overly amorous young players.

It came to her clearly that that might just be the crux of the problem with Pantier: He wasn't a rookie. Roland Pantier was a mature man, not an ambitious player a dozen years her junior.

And his interest in her was not the playful, passionless ploy of a younger man tasting his first freedom and dreaming of acclaim. No, Roland Pantier was established, mature, well known, and seven years her senior. Although his motive appeared much the same as that of a rookie—seduction for the simple sake of seduction—Elaine knew that she, at least, had responded to him on a more subtle level, with a greater need than even she could have imagined.

In a single day a man had ignited a fire within her—a fire long buried and, until the past few months, half-forgotten. But why?

Sitting in her office as the long shadows of afternoon began to fill the hall beyond, she blushed at her own curiosity and near abandon as she'd examined his legs. How could she have led herself to the brink of such indiscriminate behavior? After all, she tried to reason, his physical appearance wasn't so very much different from that of the other players she'd worked with over the years.

Or could it have been that she sensed something? Something more than pure physical desire? That question alone filled her mind as she filed records and organized her desk for the following day. What was it that had really sparked her deepest emotions? Why, even now, could she still see his face and feel the texture of his skin?

Whatever it was, she decided as she turned off the office light and closed the door behind her, must be put out of her mind and promptly. The confusion and frustration accumulated in just one day of being near him could not be allowed to continue or grow. Her effectiveness as a trainer was at stake, she told herself, but the truth was that she didn't want to face the real significance.

"Say, Doc," called red-headed Paul Rutledge as he approached her in the hallway, "want to join us for dinner? We're celebrating the start of the season."

"Who's 'we'?" she asked with a chuckle, walking toward him.

"Oh, all the rookies and a couple of us old-timers. We're going for steaks at Murphy's joint. How about it?"

His youthful zest was irresistible.

"I'll have to join you a little later," she said.

"Haven't gotten your training in for the day, huh?" Rutledge was well aware of Elaine's routine. Every evening after practice she reserved time for her own prescribed training routine.

"Nope. Are you going over right now?" They had reached the arena entrance, and she sat down to change into her skates.

"Yeah," he answered nonchalantly. "But don't worry, we won't be leaving too early. We'll wait for you!" Without waiting for an answer, he jogged away down the hallway.

The arena was still lit but eerily quiet. After a normal day of frantic activity, the cold, gigantic arena appeared rather patient and wise to Elaine. She'd always thought of the barnlike structure as having a personality all its own, and over the years she and the Omaha Ice Palace had become close, personal friends, each with her own private secrets, hopes, and dreams, each thriving on the excitement and challenge of the sport.

After moving onto the ice, Elaine slowly skated around the perimeter. Warming up and avoiding any concrete thoughts, she gained speed and tried to concentrate fully

31

on her routine. Her soulful ballet moved to music only she could hear.

Twists and turns, rapid leaps and delicate pirouettes helped her escape the day's stress and recover a sense of her own purpose.

Her five-foot five-inch body glided effortlessly as Elaine imaged how she must look on the broad expanse of ice. It was a technique she'd utilized for years. Without mirrors to perform in front of, she used a well-honed inner vision with which to monitor her style and form.

Long, shapely legs executed tightly controlled patterns over the surface, while her delicate arms fashioned expressive poses to complete the illusion of effortless precision.

Here was where she was meant to be—a part of the ice, creating her own art and at peace with life. When she skated, Elaine was lost in a world all her own, and her face, heart-shaped and glowing, reflected the tranquillity she felt.

There was no competition beyond that which she created with herself. There was no defeat, only challenge and accomplishment. Her large brown eyes, wide beneath dark, velvety lashes, danced with exhilaration as inner knowledge and keen self-assurance led to intricate demonstrations of her skill.

These were thoughts that often comforted her, and this evening, in particular, she needed a release, some comfort from the wildly emotional swings she'd experienced throughout the day.

Faster she skated, trying to rid her mind of confusion. Not even a thousand Pantiers could lead her to deceive herself; she knew intuitively who and what she was. And she could prove it—over and over—to herself, through the performance of her own brand of art. Smiling now, her face glowed with contentment.

An hour later, tired yet serene, she stepped off the ice and, for the first time, realized she had not been alone.

Roland Pantier sat on a bench next to where she'd left her coat and shoes.

"You shouldn't hide a talent like that," said Pantier quietly.

"What?" Elaine asked brusquely, more from uneasiness than from surprise.

"I said that you shouldn't hide your skating ability from the others. Do you always wait until the players are gone before taking to the ice? I mean, why skate for an empty arena? Those rookies should see what their trainer can do."

"I prefer it this way," she mumbled, sitting down on another bench and pretending to concentrate on unlacing her skates.

"Well, you ought to let those rookies see what real skate control looks like. I wish more hockey players had started out as figure skaters like you. We'd have more finesse and less fisticuffs in this game." She saw him smile but ignored the remark. His nearness agitated her, and his sudden interest in her skating was oddly disquieting.

"You skate beautifully," he said. "How long did you compete in figure skating?"

"What makes you think I was a competition skater?" Elaine replied. Still not looking at him, she fought for time to compose her reaction.

"It's obvious," he answered frankly. "And it is also quite evident that you must have been championship material." At that Elaine glanced over to catch him looking directly at her. A broad grin met her glance. "Only a champion could still skate like that," he said with a wink.

Pantier's unusual interest put Elaine on guard, but his voice and manner were no longer brash or insolent. She tried to relax and accept what he'd said as a genuine compliment. Yet the past was past, she reminded herself, and not even a tantalizing superjock could get her to discuss it. That chapter of her life was over, finished.

"I imagine you've captured quite a collection of trophies and titles," Pantier said congenially.

"Oh, I had my opportunity to shine," she replied.

"You sound as if your opportunities to shine, as you put it, are all behind you."

"Well"—she was thinking out loud—"*those* opportunities are. I guess I'm shining in a different place now." She saw him smile and look toward the rink. Apparently he realized Elaine would give no more information about her past. He didn't speak again until she had changed from her skates and stood to leave.

"Are you going to dinner at Murphy's?" he asked slowly, as if purposefully trying to sound uninterested.

"I thought I would," she answered simply. "I've been officially invited."

"So have I. Possibly we could go together."

"Possibly," she replied, feeling a little unsure of his motives but not really wanting to turn him down.

"Good. You can drive."

"Oh, so you've just invited me because I know how to get there, huh?" She chuckled, glad to have an opening to break the slight tension between them.

His laughter surprised her. "Not at all," he answered. "I don't have a car; it's in the shop for repairs."

She laughed, too, and they walked toward the parking lot. It was all so very ridiculous, she thought. Here was a man who infuriated her and charmed her almost simultaneously.

As they got into her car, she had a chance to look at him quickly. His dark eyes shone with an innocence she hadn't seen earlier.


With time nearly suspended in routine, Elaine moved through that first week of preseason training with an unnatural caution. Pantier was obviously going to be part of

34

her work life for some undetermined period, and she vowed to keep the relationship as professional as possible.

*He's just another member of the team*, she kept reminding herself—without really even trying to believe it.

Shortly before 7:00 A.M. the phone rang. Reluctant to face another Monday morning, Elaine picked up the receiver only after four insistent rings.

"Hello?"

"Up and at it! If you've got the coffee, I've got the Danish!" She recognized Meg Holloway's bubbly voice right off. "Come on, Elaine," she said proddingly. "It's almost seven. Up and at it!"

"If you say that one more time, I'll hang up." Elaine yawned as she sat up to look at the alarm clock. "By George, you're right, Meg. It is almost seven. Call me back when I wake up, say, around eight."

"Oh, come on," Meg said cajolingly. "I've made all these cinnamon Danish and don't have anyone to share them with. Now climb out of the sack and put on the coffeepot. I'm on my way." And she hung up.

There was no use fighting it. Elaine tumbled out of bed, found her robe, and trudged to the front door. She counted to nine out loud, unlocked the dead bolt, opened the door at the count of ten, and found Meg crossing the courtyard between their adjacent condos.

"What took you so long?" asked Elaine with a yawn. "I almost made it to the full count of eleven this time."

"You really are a bear in the morning," her friend answered.

"That's what they all say," replied Elaine as she followed the younger woman into her kitchen.

Elaine dragged out the coffeemaker, filled it with water and freshly ground coffee, and plugged it in, while Meg kept up a steady stream of weather and traffic reports as she cut the steaming pastry at the table.

At last they settled down to breakfast. The first cup of coffee cleared Elaine's sleepy head and started her brain functioning within minutes. Meg, who was already wide-awake and geared for action, continued to repeat the 6:00 A.M. drive time format from radio WOW, the official sports voice of the Omaha Hawks.

Right in the middle of one, particularly gloomy news bulletin, Elaine held up both hands to signal a time-out. "Enough already," Elaine said. "I know you didn't wake me up at this hour to force the morning news and a half dozen Danish down my throat. So what's going on?"

"Well, no," Meg stated confidentially. She leaned a little closer to Elaine, as if the walls were listening. "Actually I was dying to hear what's going on with you. I mean," she added, standing to pour more coffee, "you and Pantier have had dinner every night this past week. The whole world's waiting with bated breath to hear about it!"

By "the whole world" Meg meant *their* whole world: the team, the coaching staff, and dozens of admiring fans.

"So he bought me dinner once or twice. That's not exactly newsworthy, Meg."

"He bought you three dinners actually, and anything that man does while he's here is going to be news—I guarantee."

Elaine understood Meg's interest when she put it that way. As public relations and promotions director for the Hawks, Meg had the primary responsibility to keep the team in the news.

On the other hand, Meg's recap of Pantier's movements during their first week of training disturbed Elaine.

He had made a point of staying around the arena each evening until the rest of the team had left and Elaine had finished her workout. Every evening, she thought. And every evening he had offered her dinner.

The three times she accepted had been evenings when most of the hockey club was relaxing at Murphy's Pub,

36

their regular hangout during the season. She had told herself it was because she was investigating the *real* Pantier, because she was interested in how he interacted with the rookies, because she simply enjoyed being with the players. "Because," she also told herself, and anyone else who would listen, "he needed a chauffeur for a few days!"

Elaine had given herself every possible rationale for casually accepting three of his numerous invitations to dinner. But even she wasn't sure of her own reasons. Of one thing, however, she was certain: She liked being with Pantier, and that was unsettling. At Murphy's, though, she could be near him without his being too close to her.

Elaine had felt comfortable with Pantier at Murphy's. It didn't seem threatening. And it was not the least bit out of character for either one of them—separately or together—to be socializing with the rest of the players and the fans who crowded the small pub when they were there. It was safe, she'd told herself. Now Meg had made a news release out of it.

"You know, Meggan, you should be more careful with this PR spree of yours," she said cautioningly. *"Everything* Pantier does is *not* newsworthy—especially if it involves me. Now that's something *I* can guarantee."

"What's he really like?" Meg begged, apparently not listening to what Elaine was trying to get across. "You must know him better than anyone else here."

"I don't know any more about him than the players do." Elaine was momentarily pleased that she'd kept it that way. As a matter of fact, she'd purposefully shied away from any discussion with Pantier beyond last year's play-off standings. Every night she'd invited as many team members as would accept to sit with them as they ate at the pub.

It hadn't been easy either. Elaine really wanted to know about him, but she was afraid he'd sense the growing attraction she felt for him if they talked of anything more personal than his professional standing.

"That Pantier is going to increase our game attendance by bundles," she heard Meg ramble on.

"But he's not going to be playing," protested Elaine, rallying back to their conversation and away from her own fantasies. "He's here to scout, and that's official."

"I know that." Meg shrugged off the practical observation. "But he'll be dressing for all the games while he's assigned to us, and people will pay good money just to look at a superstar on the bench."

"I guess you're right," replied Elaine with some renewed interest. The fans, of course, would come, just hoping Pantier would play *part* of a period. "But we already get four to five thousand fans per game. Surely you can't expect Pantier to be worth that many more tickets."

"Of course I do. Listen, Elaine, didn't you notice how everyone at Murphy's wants his autograph or photo?" Yes, she had noticed the regular, chaotic scene.

"He just lends a certain . . . I don't know . . . *glamour* to our team, don't you think?"

"With six Adams Cup trophies to our record, I don't think the Hawks need to rely on a Pantier superstar to boost attendance." Elaine popped part of a hot Danish into her mouth and waited for Meg's rebuttal, which was swift and sure.

"Seriously, Elaine, attendance isn't going to be a problem. He'll really help the most with the team itself." Though talkative and overactive, Meg Holloway was a natural for her job; Elaine had learned to respect her opinions, even though she teased her for them.

But her odd statement made Elaine frown with curiosity. "Well, go on." She nudged Meg's arm when she didn't finish her original thought.

"I was talking to Dad the other day," she said, referring to Coach Holloway. "He wasn't at all pleased with the draft choices we were handed this season—"

"No one was," interrupted Elaine, knowing that the

38

team had been weakened by call-ups to the parent team at Edmonton and by a relatively high number of inexperienced rookies who came in after the drafts. "It's not going to be easy putting a championship team together this season."

"That's exactly what Dad said, but he believes Pantier can instill a lot of knowledge and confidence into this batch of greenhorns we're stuck with. By just having him around, Dad thinks—"

"With all due respect to your father, Meg, I don't think he can count on Roland Pantier's being much more than window dressing for the team. Believe me. I've seen enough in one short week to prove it."

Aside from their earlier skirmishes and in spite of his exacting interest in her over the past week, Elaine had watched Pantier with players and fans alike, and she was genuinely dismayed by his behavior. The younger players made no bones about idolizing him, and instead of taking their admiration as a compliment and then turning it off, Pantier encouraged the situation, often slipping into his macho jock image for hours at a time. She honestly wondered if it was his way of trying to fit in with the team or if he was just that self-assured. But she had really been afraid to get close enough to him to find out.

Pantier signed more autographs by nine o'clock each night than most of the rookie players had ever been asked for, and he insisted on spinning bright, shining yarns of the glamorous professional life well into the wee hours, knowing full well that the preseason curfew was in effect.

"So why do you hang around him?" asked Meg innocently. "You seem to be enjoying him as much as anyone."

"I hate to disillusion you, Meg, but I'm his chauffeur for the week." Although she said it with just the right amount of conviction and indignation, even Elaine wasn't convinced that this was why she'd really gone with him each

39

night. If Meg noticed the flaw in her logic, she didn't mention it.

"Oh, you're his chauffeur, huh? Then that's why he came home with you every night." Meg giggled, catching Elaine off guard.

"He didn't come home with me. I just drove him back to the complex. For heaven's sake, Meggan Holloway, don't try to make headlines with some trumped-up romance between that French Panther and me."

Elaine stood and began clearing cups and dishes from the table with a great show of regal indignation.

"But you did drive him home, didn't you?" Meg persisted innocently. "I'll have another cup of coffee."

"The coffee shop is closed. And yes, I drove him home. We *all* live here at Glenwood, Meg. Or haven't you noticed?"

Elaine looked at Meg to discover her chuckling, and she herself began to laugh.

"I think this lady's protesting a bit too much," Elaine said, pouring them both another cup of coffee.

"Yep, I think so," Meg said with a giggle. "And in case you haven't noticed it yet, your face is a dead giveaway. You don't fool me one bit. You like him, don't you, Elaine? And how does Pantier feel?"

"Oh, he really likes me. Ask your father; he nearly seduced me in the coach's office as we were being introduced."

The image Elaine's statement conjured up in her mind was so forceful that she quickly sat down to steady her trembling legs.

"Don't you find that terribly exciting, Elaine—I mean, really? Big-league player, falling head over heels . . ." Meg went on, oblivious to Elaine's reaction to the conversation.

"Listen, Meg, you haven't been around this sort of life as long as I have." Elaine turned suddenly quite serious in an attempt to control the conversation and its effect on her. "There are three kinds of men in professional athletics—"

"I know, I know," Meg interrupted. "There's the marrying kind, who play for a living; then there's the never-marring kind, who live for playing; and then there's the kind who—"

"Who use their celebrity status—married or not—to take advantage of the women who idolize them." Elaine finished the statement in dead earnest.

"See, you think I never pay any attention to what you say," Meg said rebukingly. "What type is Pantier, Madame Expert?"

"I don't know really," Elaine said, trying to give him the benefit of the doubt, "but I'm afraid he appears to be a number two from my initial evaluation. He lives just to play hockey. And I'm not too sure he doesn't border on being a number three. So don't try to make a thing between us, Meg. I just want to see him return to Edmonton as soon as possible."

While she believed what she'd just told Meggan, Elaine felt a rush of vague guilt. Remembering Saturday night at Murphy's and how Pantier had actually worked in a number of stories about his own trainer at Edmonton, just to pull Elaine into direct, positive conversation with both players and fans alike, she wondered if her evaluation of him wasn't somewhat off base.

"That doesn't sound quite like you, Elaine. Where's the den mother in you?" Meg asked. "Usually you take more interest in a player. Don't you want to know what makes Pantier tick? I mean, really *tick?*"

Den mother—two words Elaine had heard far too often lately. It made her sound like a fussy old maid, living out her life through others' accomplishments, and she said so to Meggan.

"I meant it as a compliment, really," Meg retorted. "But aren't you just a little concerned for yourself? For as long as

41

I can remember, you've lived for this team and for skating. Isn't there something in your life besides hockey and skating? Why, even in off-season," she blurted, "you teach power skating or brood around the swimming pool. You only come alive when the season starts. . . . I'll bet it's been two years since you've had a real date."

Meg stopped lecturing abruptly; she'd gone much farther with her well-meant criticism than she had planned, and the faraway look in Elaine's eyes told her she might have hurt, more than helped, her dearest friend.

Fortunately the phone rang, and Meg was rescued from the delicate situation she'd created. As Elaine answered the call, Meg picked up the remaining Danish, waved a silent farewell, and retreated through the front door with a muffled bang.

## CHAPTER THREE

Elaine's mind was still whirling from Meg's comments as she numbly answered the phone. Only after the caller had spoken for a full minute or more did she even recognize the voice on the other end as belonging to Phil Walters, the assistant coach.

He plodded through the long list of exercises and weight-training recommendations she had given him on Friday and seemed not to notice that she seldom commented except when he asked direct questions. Her mind was still glued to Meg's parting commentary, and she was relieved when Phil didn't press for an extended conversation. After she had assured him of her reasoning and added a few additional ideas to the schedule, he ended with a hearty "See you later, Doc!" and hung up.

It was just a little after eight; she was due at the arena around ten. But her enthusiasm had been dimmed significantly by Meg's accurate evaluation of the state of her life over the past two years.

Slowly she walked back through the living room and wandered to the large picture window overlooking one of Glenwood's many ponds and wide, rolling lawns, dotted with majestic trees, that fanned out over the ten-acre condominium complex.

What was so bad about her life? she wondered. Or was it that Meg—younger, impressionable, and incurably romantic—wasn't experienced enough to see the beauty and stability that surrounded Elaine's career? What she did with the Hawks was meaningful. But, then, she knew that Meg had not been questioning her career; she had seen only its transparency.

Meggan Holloway was only twenty-six, Elaine mentally acknowledged, but she had a lot more insight into some things than Elaine had had at that age. "Meggan's right, fellows," she said aloud, using the clutter of potted plants in and around the window as her audience. "We can't go on like this. We have to get back to life and living one of these days."

Idly she picked over the plants, pulling a dead leaf here and dusting a waxy stem there, all the while remembering that special quality of wholeness her life had once held.

Pacing across the deep-pile carpeting that accented the room's earth tone with burnt sienna decor, she watered the flowers and absently fluffed the sofa cushions. Without really seeing the room, Elaine busied herself. The quicker her mind brought back past scenes, the faster she worked.

Had it only been three years now since she and Tony first bought this condo and spent every spare moment painting and decorating it? So long yet just a short time really. Elaine stopped pacing and really looked at the spacious room. Tony's watercolors dotted the walls. All cheerful, earthy pictures.

The old platform rocker that they refinished together, with the needlepoint cover she'd designed and sewn, stood silently in the corner near the window. It had been a favorite spot, where Tony sat and dozed away long winter afternoons, watching the trees grow heavy with snow and dreaming of being called up to Edmonton.

They both knew his turn would come. An outstanding goalie, Tony had to wait only until one of the coveted positions at Edmonton was vacated. When one of the two contract goalies was finally retired, they both knew that his amazing record would carry him right up to major-league standing.

Together they waited. As head trainer, Elaine traveled with the team throughout the year. She and Tony were never separated. Being together made his waiting easier, he had always said. Their marriage revolved around a mutual respect for the sport; their love centered on achieving Tony's dream.

Elaine moved into the kitchen and found herself staring out another window. Among the clusters of low brick condos there was the usual morning activity. Players one by one appeared, packing practice gear into their car trunks and playfully horsing with each other on the grass. She looked at the clock. It was nearly nine, but she couldn't pull herself away from the window, even though she knew she would be late if she didn't hustle.

Memories were coming in rapid succession now. She could not interrupt their replay until the final scene. Having tried before to shut off the newsreel of her mind, Elaine accepted the fact that once she had allowed it to start, she had no choice but to finish it.

Watching a few of the Hawks preparing to leave for practice, she remembered how young and idealistic she and Tony had been. That he was still waiting for his break into the majors at twenty-nine never fazed him. "There's plenty of time," he would say. "After all, a goalie doesn't burn out as fast as the others." Elaine knew, even then, that they were being unrealistic, but it didn't really matter. Only the dream had any meaning. And just as they believed, his call finally came.

In midseason an Edmonton goalie broke his ankle, and Tony left on three hours' notice to take his place. The moment they'd waited for years for arrived without much fanfare. A late-night phone call from Cap Holloway, the hasty packing of his valise, an early-morning drive to the airport, and he was gone forever.

The last time Elaine saw him alive was as he played his first game in the major league. Clustered around a single TV, she and most of his old teammates watched the action on cable.

He was killed that same night: a car accident as he drove back to the hotel.

She remembered the phone call, all the details, and, finally, the last scene from her memory as they buried him on a bitterly cold February morning. It was over—the replay of her past. She sighed, still watching the players appear one by one outside her window, but there were no tears.

Their bitter fate had long ago been resolved; the grief and mourning were over. She had accepted it as part of life; just how she'd been able to, Elaine didn't know. But she no longer cried at the memory.

As Meg had aptly pointed out, she had to stop denying the inevitable reality of returning to life and the living: a life beyond old, faded memories.

Meg had hit it with true accuracy when she'd said that Elaine came alive only during the hockey season. Strange how Elaine hadn't seen it herself. Or had she—only to repress the implication?

For some unexplainable reason Meg's evaluation had forced Elaine to see what she had created after Tony's death. Her life alone was sheltered by her work and all-consuming allegiance to Cap and the team. It was safe, warm, and familiar. Being an integral part of the Hawks kept her mind occupied. Only during the summer break, when there was no routine, no work, to distract her, did Elaine become restless and withdrawn.

Meg was right. She lived for skating and the team. Little else mattered. Nothing else seemed to interest her. That is, nothing until Pantier appeared. But she didn't want to think about that, and she forced herself to block him out of her mind.

As she wandered away from the kitchen window and walked into her bedroom, Elaine remembered the simple philosophy she and Tony had lived by: "Life's only worth what you're willing to put into it!" It was plain, direct, and all-encompassing, but she had somehow forgotten to apply its reasoning to her life after Tony had gone.

"Well, I won't forget again," she murmured as she laid out a cool mint green warm-up suit and stuffed her gym bag with the usual assortment of paraphernalia. *Tony would be terribly disappointed if he knew I'd stopped loving all of life,* she thought.

Elaine stopped and looked over the clean, warm lines of the antiques-furnished bedroom. Focusing on the wide oak bed that Tony had chosen, she expected a sudden rush of memory to engulf her.

She waited. The rush never came. It was the final sign she needed to be certain that the past had actually become the past.

Relieved by an inner assurance, Elaine took a deep breath, squared her shoulders, and headed for the shower.

A truth had surfaced from the deep darkness of her mind: Elaine was afraid to face the future. Fear of the future—she had finally recognized it.

*That* was it. Fear was trying to trick her into believing that life held no meaningful future without Tony. She realized it wasn't true; even Tony would have agreed with her.

As she showered and dressed, Elaine explored her feelings about Roland Pantier to discover another truth about herself. That odd form of anger he'd managed to trigger was not really anger at all. He frightened her. Not that he had tried to, but she knew that his intensity and their mutual fascination had reawakened a half-forgotten energy, an urgency inside her. And the powerful physical attraction she felt, after two long years of emptiness, had been truly frightening.

She dressed quickly, feeling much more optimistic about

the day. Another unreasonable fear had been named, and it wasn't called Roland Pantier. Not at all, she mused. It was the fear of risking. She was afraid of getting close to any man with the capability of striking a strong emotional need in her. She was afraid to risk another intimate relationship, even simple friendship, with a man her own age.

Elaine had a way of coping with life's uncertainties. Each time she realized that a new fear had seized her, she named it. Fear, she thought, was a dragon in her mind— some unreal fantasy that had outgrown its true proportions, something that could be seen, named, and ultimately conquered.

Two fear dragons had been named in a single day, she realized. But once they had been named and recognized, their power to manipulate her life was greatly diminished.

How ridiculous to fear the future and a simple need like risking, she thought, as she headed toward the arena, already ten minutes late for practice. She had known men just like Pantier, none of them nicknamed the Panther, granted, but nearly all of them had turned out to be pretty regular guys in the end. Her wanting to be near him, and taking the opportunity as it had been offered, could be only a sign that somehow he was meant to help her overcome a fear. If only she'd listen more closely to the clues her mind gave her, she thought. Confusion and conflict would be much less traumatic.

So she'd risk a friendship with this Panther person, just as she had with other players over the years. Maybe if she were less defensive, he would be less aggressive. Elaine knew she had to try. Now that she had the dragons named, she meant to slay them, one by one, once and for all. And Roland Pantier might be the key.

It was almost ten thirty when she arrived at Cap Holloway's office for the regular Monday morning staff meeting.

The door to his office was open as usual, and she bounded in, full of good humor, sure she was the last to arrive.

"Good morning, Cap!" she said cheerfully, pulling a chair across the narrow room toward his desk. "And how is the Super Hawk this lovely morning?" Elaine sat down, crossed her legs, propped her clipboard against the edge of the desk, and tried to look as if she weren't running a full half hour late.

Holloway smiled and leaned back in his swivel chair. "You tell me, Doc. How *should* the Super Hawk feel? After all, you've been working with the new flock for a whole week."

She leaned across the desk and viewed him with mock sincerity. "Well, Cap, this flock has Hawk potential, but right now I'd say they have about as much grace and finesse as a gaggle of geese."

Holloway chuckled and winked at her. "What do you think about that, Roland?"

"Can't agree or disagree," replied Pantier in a deep, smooth voice, and Elaine turned to look at him. As she turned, he rose from where he had been sitting near the door and pulled his chair closer to the desk. "I haven't really gotten a good look at the team yet," he went on. As he sat down, his knee and thigh brushed against Elaine's leg. Cap's desk was not designed to accommodate two wide chairs with broad padded arms.

Although she smiled and nodded as Pantier commented, the unexpected contact sent shock waves, reminiscent of their first encounters, pounding through her. *Calm down*, she commanded her body, and the pulsing diminished to a more comfortable sensation of warm, tingling excitement. *Better. Much better*, she thought, not hearing a word of additional conversation that passed between Pantier and Holloway.

"What do you think, Elaine?" Cap Holloway's voice sounded far away.

"Better," she said, repeating her thoughts aloud before realizing it.

The confused look on the coach's face told her she'd committed quite a faux pas.

"I'm sorry," she said, blushing slightly. "I must not have heard your question."

Holloway looked amused as he continued to bob back and forth in his swivel chair. "Roland seems to think the team has a lot of potential, but that it's pulling in opposite directions."

"That's probably true," Elaine said quickly, recovering her composure. "But it's not unusual for a new team to have coordination problems."

"I don't think it's just coordination," said Pantier with honest interest. "They seem to be lacking a real desire to cooperate with one another, or so Phil Walters has been telling me."

"Elaine?" Holloway threw the observation back to her for comment.

"Okay. But then Phil's been working with them in game plays; he would have a better view." She found herself looking comfortably at Pantier, absorbed in the question and pleased with his interest. "Still, we do have a lot of rookies this season and only six holdovers. It's always hard to get everyone calmed down and working as a unit with so many fresh, inexperienced players. After the final cuts at Edmonton we should have five more men with some working experience, and that'll improve things."

"That *would* help," Pantier replied evenly. "But Cap just got word that the Hawks are getting seven more rookies; they'll be in this afternoon." Elaine was surprised at his genuine concern; Pantier emphasized it with a wistful, knowing nod that sent his thick hair falling across his forehead.

"It doesn't appear all that promising," the coach finally commented. "It's going to be very difficult to maintain our league standings this year with so many green recruits on the roster."

Silence replaced conversation, as each sat thinking of the probabilities. Now, with only one week left before regulation play began, the coaching staff had had its job doubled in complexity.

There had already been five weeks of total evaluation. The first two occurred at Edmonton, where all the players —major-leaguers, seasoned minor-leaguers, and recruited rookies—worked out en masse before the first cut was made. Then came another two weeks at St. Cloud, with both the Edmonton minor teams working out to determine yet a second round of cuts.

Now, halfway through the final two-week session at home, the Hawks awaited the arrival of the last players to be sent down from Edmonton—those rookies cut from major-league consideration after a concentrated workout during the second two-week session in Canada. Unfortunately the Hawks would have to handle a much higher ratio of rookies this season: twelve out of twenty players.

Phil Walters arrived as they sat in silence, pulled up yet another chair, and joined the group of somber people clustered around Coach Holloway's desk.

"Let me guess," he said. "You're all thinking about the good news from Edmonton."

"That's right, Phil. Any ideas?" Holloway asked as he lit a cigar before resuming a pensive wobble in his chair.

"Just one, and it's kind of obvious," he answered. "We have to get Roland here into the position of player coach immediately. He can do a lot to turn those greenhorn, hotshot rookies into hockey players."

"I appreciate the compliment, Phil," said Pantier warily. "But I don't intend to be here long enough to make any significant contribution."

"You'll be here for a while," Elaine spoke up, bristling at the fact that he was still denying the truth of his situation.

51

"That is, unless you've done some super superstar scouting over the weekend."

Pantier turned to give her a long, devilish grin and accented it with a wink. "You underestimate me, Miss D'Arte. I'm really amazing when given a chance."

Rather than blush, Elaine felt like laughing. The remark fitted him perfectly, and he said it with such conviction that she wondered how he could have ever intimidated her. Roland had confidence and a zeal for his profession that she had to admire, even if his constant innuendos made it hard to see at times.

"Okay," she answered with a wink of her own. "We all agree that you're amazing. And with that in mind, I'd like to agree with Phil. I like his idea, and I've seen how the players"—not wanting to use the appropriate word, Elaine hesitated before adding—"look up to you." And then to Holloway and Walters, she added, "I'll agree to getting Pantier on the ice."

"You know, Roland, as long as you're assigned to the Hawks, your official title is supposed to be player coach," Cap Holloway went on with an easy voice which did not reflect the fact that he was actually issuing a mandate to Pantier. "I think we're all in agreement here that you'll make a real contribution in that slot no matter how long you stay. A month, two, maybe three." He glanced at Phil Walters, who nodded an affirmative. "I'll let Edmonton know what we plan to do and get a clearance for you to skate with the team if required. With all of us working on these rookies, we just might be able to shape this group up into a strong hockey team before long. What do you think?"

Pantier's mouth firmed, and as it did, the black fringe of his mustache formed a thoughtful curve about his full, wide lips.

"I'll do what I can in the time we have." His eyes flickered with a second thought. "Perhaps these young men *can* benefit from my experience. Yes?"

The question was posed to Elaine, whom he looked to for a response. She steadied herself and smiled.

"Only your on-ice experience, please," she replied. "We don't need too many more evenings like the ones we've been having at Murphy's this past week. And that's an order from your trainer!"

"That's right," said Holloway lazily. "Celebrating's fine, but I want these boys to be working hard over the next week. So curfew's eleven o'clock. With hard work and effort, they'll really have a reason to celebrate as we get into the season."

There were only four working days before Edmonton arrived for the last preseason exhibition game scheduled for Friday night, and they all were concerned about the team's chances.

"I can't see that we'll be able to do much," Phil said complainingly. "Even with Roland working on them, four days just isn't enough to get a crew moving." Phil was expressing everyone's thoughts. It was particularly important that the Hawks make at least a decent attempt at playing well against their parent team.

"None of us expects a win, of course," Cap said. "But there's got to be *some* show for the fans." He said "fans," but everyone knew he really meant the owners, who always came in for the exhibition games. Holloway wanted the Hawks to prove they were worth all the money Edmonton spent to keep a farm team in Omaha.

"Well," said Pantier suddenly, "then they will have to skate hard. What they lack in skill will have to be made up in power."

"They're not too powerful either," said Elaine. "The whole lot of them move way too slowly on the ice."

"So you concur, eh?" Pantier questioned her with a grin. "Maybe we've found common ground after all." His comment had a separate meaning from the one Cap and Phil picked up on, and Elaine tried not to show she alone had understood him.

"Roland has a point." Holloway's chair wobbled more as he thought about the problem. "Our players have always been a little too polite." He told them about a sportswriter who had described the team's style. " 'All an opponent has to do is ask for the puck politely enough, and a Hawk will pass it over to him,' " he quoted. "Never will forget that. Still burns me to think of it."

They all laughed, but each knew it was really true.

"Then I think the place to start is with some old-fashioned aggressive playing. What do you think, Roland?" Phil pressed on, following Cap's line of reasoning.

"It can't hurt. We all have to learn to play with the big boys sometimes; isn't that right Miss D'Arte?" Roland's second innuendo slipped by everyone but Elaine. But she was learning his game. This time she didn't hesitate to rush him.

"Only the rookies," she answered. "The rest of us know what the game is all about."

To her surprise Pantier flushed a warm pink and didn't reply as Cap continued with renewed enthusiasm.

"Good. We're all in agreement. Starting today, I want the emphasis to be on speed and handling." But he was more specific to Pantier. "Roland, I want you to work with both Phil and Elaine, but no rough stuff. We can't have you getting injured. Is that okay with everyone?"

"The workout will be good for him," Elaine said.

Pantier concurred, and the meeting was adjourned.

The Hawks were now on a standard schedule: Any day that they didn't play a game would be spent in a grueling afternoon workout. Mornings were spent at the gym. Wednesdays were free days. And most of the games would be played from Thursdays through Sundays.

Elaine left the meeting, and instead of having lunch, she

54

went straight to her office to prepare a new series of power skating drills. Although her thoughts constantly returned to Pantier, she was somehow able to draft the complicated drills before the players arrived back at the arena that afternoon.

Fighting a fear dragon was one thing; fantasizing over Pantier's lusty dialogue was quite another. She had to force herself back into the mold of trainer again.

The newest batch of rookies was a difficult lot. She knew how disheartened they all were at being on Edmonton's cut list, and their disgruntled reactions to being stuck back in the minor league were apparent as she tried to organize the full team of twenty into the more difficult drills she'd set for that session.

Instead of having each player individually maneuver the obstacle maze of tumbling barriers and pylons, she divided the players into ten pairs and issued hockey sticks and practice pucks to all.

"Each pair of you will work as a single unit on this," she explained. "Start out passing the puck to each other around the pylons. When you come to a barrier, pass the puck to your mate on the left, somersault over the barrier, and pick up the puck again. At the next barrier pass it off to the right, and your mate will take the barrier."

The instructions were complex; the drill was terribly intricate and demanding. Even Elaine grew anxious when she saw Pantier trudge into the arena and sit down at the players' bench to watch. Tension spread over the ice like a thick haze.

Not one of the paired players could effectively coordinate the drill. They fell over one another and the obstacles with little regard for technique or precision, and Elaine became more agitated with each new attempt.

"Slow down!" she shouted. "Work that puck back and forth! Look ahead of you! Use those skates to control!"

Nothing she said worked. No one was paying attention to the basics; everyone was angry, and the anger showed.

Not all the players even made it through the first round of the drill. She stopped them after several had fallen and even more had begun to catcall and grumble.

"Hold it! Hold it!" she shouted. "What's your problem?" Elaine asked the question of the whole group standing before her.

"What good is all this anyway?" one of the new rookies had the gall to shout. "I came here to play hockey, not be an Olympic gymnast."

Before she could answer, Pantier skated up beside her. "What's your name?" he demanded of the rookie.

"Boykin!"

"Fine, Boykin. You want to play hockey? Pro hockey, maybe?" Pantier said in an even but thundering tone. "Then you'd better learn how to control not only those skates but your body as well. And Miss D'Arte's just the one to teach you."

"I got control," shouted another rookie.

"Oh, you do, eh? You can skate like this?" Without further comment, he took Elaine into his arms. "Waltz time," he whispered and then moved her into a paired figure skating position and began.

For several seconds Elaine simply glided, never feeling the ice beneath her and completely oblivious to the world. Her body molded itself to Pantier's form, soft and pliable against his hard frame. His scent was mysteriously heady, and he held her against the heat of his body with one enormous arm. Her left hand rested easily on his shoulder, and she was fascinated by the way his muscles rippled beneath her touch. Her right hand was enclosed in Roland's; his large fingers wrapped about hers so snugly that she felt his pulse throbbing against her palm. But this time the electricity between them did not snap and crackle as before. Rather, it drew them together and raced around them with incredible voltage. Like opposite poles of a magnet, they met and held together.

Pantier moved in long, graceful sweeps, carrying her along. Their bodies met, then momentarily separated, and she touched the hardness of him. That overpowering magnetism held them together, then drew them apart. Helpless in its grip, Elaine didn't fight its command.

This man in her arms was not the bruised and rugged hockey player who teased and cajoled her. Elaine knew that this was the real Pantier she held: large but gentle; powerful yet tender. She now skated with the man, not the image. She knew his true identity—the essence of his inner spirit—as he held her safely above the ice.

He moved faster. She clung to him and felt his leg push against hers. Then he held her out, just above the ice in a slow, gentle spin.

The cold surface of the rink rushed past her prone body, yet it had no effect on the raging flame he'd kindled within her.

He stopped to meet her, and they both turned together, ever closer to the ice. As he touched the length of her and glided beside her, Elaine was hypnotized by desire. The strength of his arms, the fresh smell of musk, mixed with exertion, and his body's heat all covered her at once. She was ablaze with longing. He'd set her afire there on the ice.

*Oh, how wonderfully you move, Pantier,* she thought. *How could I have ever feared you?* her mind whispered to him as their eyes met.

Elaine realized how little she really knew about this man. Still, she knew enough. There was no need to restrain her feelings any longer. The fear had dissolved completely, and in its place she'd found confidence and trust in him.

Roland was smiling as he moved upright once more and pulled her back to him. As if they'd skated together a million times before and known each other's timing by heart, she reached around his neck and felt her body rise

57

off the ice in another long, sweeping spin. He held her only by the waist, but Elaine felt completely safe. She trusted him completely, while longing for that brief moment to last forever. Only that indescribable sensation of freedom, form, and fire mattered.

All too soon it was over. She felt him squeeze her firmly and brush her with his lips before breaking the invisible bond between them.

"So you think you can skate?" she listened to him say. "Well, when you can skate like that, I'll believe it!"

He skated past her and left the rink.

Somehow Elaine managed to complete the session. Just how she never remembered.

## CHAPTER FOUR

After their intense encounter on the ice it was easier for Elaine to be near Pantier. She sorted through the many reasons for the change, but during the week that followed, Elaine was able to reduce it all to a few simple explanations: She respected his skill, she understood his need to compete, and after all other reasoning had died away, she accepted the fact that she wanted him. Desperately.

He had made her aware just how much she missed the feel of a man. The life she'd created for herself lacked one very important ingredient: a man of her own age with whom she could share herself, body and soul. Pantier had vividly reminded her of that missing element.

Alive and dynamic, he had found the key to her memory, and when she remembered what had been forgotten, fear and trepidation disappeared. In their place she found desire. Elaine wanted to hold him, to have him, and to know him. She needed to discover every fiber of Roland, the Panther.

Passionate curiosity was easier to manage than fear, so it was easier to be near him. Still, she refused to pursue Roland openly. It simply wasn't her nature, and there was nothing she could do to change that. It was a minor frustration that she handled well, all the while praying that his interest in her was just as overwhelming as hers was in him.

Autumn faded with the last week of practice. Bright hues of warm red and gold disappeared from the trees; the early

October air had turned icy with bone-chilling drizzle by midweek. Yet the weather had little effect on any of them as the atmosphere of the arena grew more frenzied with each passing day.

After Roland's gallant assist Elaine had no problems whatsoever with the power skating sessions. In fact, the players worked even harder than she demanded, inspired by Pantier's example.

"They're warmed up for you," she said to Roland after a session.

"I've been watching," he said. "I think they've got the idea anyway." Without another word, he went to work.

She grew disappointed as his playfulness subsided more with every passing day of practice. He'd taken Cap's direction, and all his energy appeared focused on the team and the exhibition game with Edmonton.

"I want them to make a good showing," he told her one morning as Elaine routinely taped his ankles before practice began. "After all, if I have to be down here, I want my mates at Edmonton to know I'm working, not just loafing the season away."

"Do you really think they're worried about your loafing?" she asked.

"Yeah," he grumbled as she applied the gauze and tape. "They probably think I'm having a good time. I'm not really earning my keep, that's for sure!"

"I wouldn't say that," she said, marveling at how naturally they communicated now. "You're working plenty hard, and the team's beginning to show it."

"That's okay, I guess," he answered. She knew that his mind wasn't really on the Hawks when he added, "But I can't very well help Edmonton win another Stanley Cup by playing nursemaid to a bunch of rookies in Omaha."

She didn't continue questioning him. She knew his motivation. Pantier was isolated from *his* world, and his objections grew louder with every day he wasn't playing.

Intuitively Elaine knew what was in Roland's mind. He was working the Hawks hard to show Edmonton that he was still a valuable asset, still a superstar. Roland was trying to prove himself and to stall his inevitable retirement. He wouldn't accept it. Elaine read it in his every action. He probably would never accept the end of his pro career, and it hurt her to watch his futile efforts. Only the Hawks would benefit from his zeal, she thought. And in the end Roland would be left alone and unrewarded.

Elaine watched as he worked the team hard but not unfairly. Roland expected them to play even though he couldn't. Perhaps, she thought, he was trying to get them to play *for* him, to become an extension of his prowess on the ice. And *that* she understood completely.

The hours spent in scrimmage became rougher as the week progressed. It had become her habit to watch the exhausting sessions that Phil and Roland engineered. They went well beyond Cap's notion of speed and puck handling, and Elaine became concerned that Pantier's frustration was pushing him to stress an inordinate level of body contact.

Her opportunity to confront the problem came on Wednesday, when Paul Rutledge became the target of Vosienne's counterchecking elbow.

"How is he?" Roland asked as he entered her office. Paul had just left, bruised and aching but unharmed.

"It could have been a lot worse, Roland. Just a little harder, and Vosienne would have broken his nose. This slap shot hockey has got to go." She made her point and stood staring at him for a response.

"You're overreacting, Doc. It's all part of the game, and they'd better learn it now. Rutledge will protect himself better next time. In the long run there will be fewer injuries after they—"

"After they're goons!" She glared at him again. Elaine hated to think that the Hawks could become brutal, mindless hockey goons, who spent more game time fighting than playing genuine hockey.

"The Hawks aren't going to become goons," he answered in a patient tone. "I don't believe in that approach. I just want to teach them as much as I can while I'm here."

Those great dark eyes beckoned her to reason with him.

"Listen, Roland, why don't you teach them what you know best? Those young men need to know how to work as a unit, a team. And no amount of power skating or defensive rough stuff is going to replace strong teamwork. They respect you, you know. Show them how *you* got to be a superstar."

She wanted to hug him and tell him that she understood how badly he wanted to play and how hard it must be for him to watch the action. She wanted to, but she didn't. Words, and words alone, were their only form of exchange.

He smiled at her and winked. "Your logic is impeccable," he answered in French. She didn't comprehend what he'd said, but she knew he'd agreed.

"Ah, and what do we have here?" Roland asked, changing the subject skillfully. He'd picked up an opened letter from Elaine's desk and stood before her, reading it with unabashed interest. His curiosity was so guileless that Elaine couldn't be angry. "It seems you have quite a reputation, Doc."

"Yep," Elaine answered, as she pulled the letter from his hand. "My reputation has spread all the way from Omaha to Indianapolis. Remarkable, isn't it?" She quickly folded the single page and slid it back into its original envelope.

"You shouldn't joke about that kind of offer, Elaine," Roland went on more seriously. "The Sports Medicine Center is top-notch; it's looking for only the very best, you know. When are you going to interview for the job?"

"Never," she replied flatly while organizing the desktop with indifference.

"Why not?" Pantier pried. "Offers like that aren't made every day."

"No." She chuckled. "They're made about once a month or so. I get a letter from Dr. Caswell pretty regularly, and if I ever decide to hide away in some sterile medical center, I'll take him up on the offer. But right now I'm too busy trying to keep this hockey team in shape. Now, out! The doctor's busy." She playfully pushed him toward the office door and opened it for him. "Next?" she shouted into the empty hallway beyond.

Pantier just laughed and shook his head as he left.

And so the week moved on, filled with hard work during the day and little to distract her from thinking of Pantier at night. But it was comforting to know that she'd been right. The less fearful she was of him, the less aggressive he became. The fear dragon had been conquered, and in its place a need had materialized. Elaine no longer feared intimacy with Pantier; she longed for it.

The Friday afternoon session was short; it was more a pep rally than a workout. Cap talked at length about the team's progress. For once he pumped them up and sounded as if they'd become overnight wonders. The team *had* worked hard, and the players deserved to feel good about their efforts a few hours before the exhibition game. But the coaching staff knew the truth. Their progress hadn't been that significant, especially considering that Edmonton would be their first opponent.

"They just aren't functioning as a team yet," Elaine said to Pantier as they left the arena and walked toward the parking lot.

"I know, but you expect too much, too soon." They had reached Elaine's car and stood talking in the fall wind. "You can't just bring a group of players together and expect them to function automatically as a team." She knew he was right; they shared a common viewpoint. But it delighted her to have him actively prolong their conversation.

"The six players who have worked together before can't compensate for twelve rookies," he continued, leaning against the car door. "It takes quite awhile for people to settle in and start understanding how to relate to one another."

His eyes bored right through her, and instantly she knew he was talking about more than just the Hawks.

"You're right," she answered, wanting to play the game that was becoming a ritual between them. "Sometimes you have two players who are so competitive that they actually work against each other, never realizing how much they could gain if they only pulled together in one direction."

Roland's brow arched as he smiled down at her. *"Exactement,"* he said in French, then added in English, "And when the moment comes when they see how ridiculous it has all been, they stop competing and discover how marvelous it is to be on the same team."

She wanted to answer him, but her throat was dry. Her voice abandoned her while she stood just looking at him. They had finally found a way to acknowledge their mutual attraction. Feeling slightly foolish but not really caring, she swam in the dark pools of his eyes and smiled, almost wantonly, at his suggestion. Somehow there was nothing negative or unnatural about the moment; his nearness, his smile —it was perfect.

Surely this wasn't the Roland Pantier who had appeared in Cap's office just a few short weeks before. Yes, this beautiful dark man vaguely resembled the other, but he was so different, so human and sensitive.

His eyes were still intense, but now she sensed a tenderness in them as well. And the strong body that towered above her was inviting, no longer intimidating. Oh, how this panther had changed, she thought. And the change made him only that much more tempting.

Elaine felt Roland's bare hand against her cheek; his warm fingers cradled her face and moved slowly, in tiny circles, across her flesh. His touch sent ripples through her entire being, and she shivered with delight.

"You must be cold," he said. He opened the car door and helped her in. "Are you going to be at Murphy's after the game?"

"I wouldn't miss it," she almost whispered. "Why, do you still need a ride?" It seemed a suitable conclusion, and the logical statement made her sound more composed than she really was.

"I can ride with Phil or Cap," he replied, and then he winked. "But I would rather go with you. I'd like you to meet my mates on the Edmonton team. They're a burly lot, but you'll like them."

"Fine," Elaine answered, and it was settled.

With less than three hours to go before game time, she hurried away, leaving him standing there alone. She wondered, only briefly, if she had misunderstood his meaning. Then she dismissed the thought entirely. Only a fool could deny what he'd meant.

It should have been just like any other preseason exhibition game. Elaine had experienced it all before: the rock music bouncing through the halls; the bustle of excited fans; the crowing of hallway vendors as they hawked programs and souvenirs, everything from counterfeit team shirts to hockey puck paperweights. The light scent of buttered popcorn rose in the cool air and mingled with the piercing blasts of the arena organist, who pumped out his standard medley of pop hits from a catwalk high above the rink. But it wasn't the same at all *this* opening night.

The circus hype and hustle greeted her like a long-lost friend, and she found herself smiling contentedly as the color of life and the living hummed all around her.

Running late, she cruised through the spirited crowd of

spectators in the outer hall, her gym bag slung over her shoulder and a wide, excited grin on her face. Everything seemed new and fresh, just like the very first game she'd ever worked. That was years ago. She thought she'd grown used to the feeling, the energy, the anticipation.

But the last week had unwrapped all kinds of memories, not the least of them being a bright, optimistic excitement about this season.

After pushing through the dense throng of fans waiting impatiently outside the players' dressing rooms and past Cap's cubbyhole, Elaine sprinted the last few feet to her own office. Although she couldn't see through the forest of bodies, she knew the fans were waiting for a chance to see Roland and the other Edmonton players as well as the new Hawks lineup. She understood their rapture; she felt it herself, but for reasons far removed from autographs and adulation.

She unlocked the door and flipped on the light, then threw her bag on the floor and began to change. With just fifteen minutes left before the game began, she quickly struggled out of her jeans and sweater and hastily pulled on her official trainer's uniform. The black fleece warm-up suit, embroidered with a large gold Hawks emblem and name patch, was warm and soft against her body and sent yet another anxious message to her mind, another familiar indication that indeed, a new season of her life had really begun.

As she slipped on heavy socks and tied her black sneakers, Roland tottered through the door on his skates and surprised her.

"Whew, I thought I locked that!" Elaine gasped.

"Glad you didn't," he said, trying to maneuver the padded carpeting on the thin steel blades of his skates. "Had a heck of a time getting through that crowd." In black knee-length shorts and long striped shirt, trimmed in yellow-gold, complete with thick wide-shoulder and leg padding, he was an imposing sight. The skates gave him added height; the padding accented his muscular body to extraordinary proportions.

"You look gorgeous in black, Roland," Elaine said as she tried not to let him see the way he really affected her. "Black goes so well with your eyes." She chuckled.

"Yeah, very sleek, huh?" He walked toward her and began to pull his jersey up. Elaine just stood motionless, not certain what he had in mind. "Got a little something for you," he finally said, pulling a regulation referee's shirt out from under his jersey.

"Where did you get this?" She laughed as he handed it to her. "Oh, Roland, you didn't—"

"He'll never miss it. Must have had a dozen of them in his suitcase." The referee's dressing room was adjacent to the players', and Pantier had made a small "requisition" while no one was watching. "I want you to wear it under your sweat suit. If the going gets rough, we're going to need all the help we can get!" His face beamed at his own prank, and Elaine could do nothing else but laugh with him.

"You're crazy, Roland!" she sputtered. "Where's my whistle?"

"Oh, almost forgot." He reached down into his over-the-knee socks, produced a ref's whistle, complete with chain, and put it over her head. "He must have had two dozen of these!"

Elaine stood mesmerized but still giggling at his unorthodox gift.

Without warning Roland pulled her into his arms. His full, warm mouth covered hers instantly, and he kissed Elaine tenderly. For a brief, wild moment they melted together. Their bodies blended into one as they had that afternoon on the ice. The air was still now, but the energy between them was the same, and Elaine was overcome by its effect.

All too suddenly it was over, and Pantier turned to leave. "Almost forgot the real reason I came in here," he said, opening the door.

"What? What else?" she gasped. Her knees were threatening to fold beneath her.

"Are we still on for the party after the game?"

"Sure," she answered as calmly as she could.

"Good. Will you wait for me outside the dressing room?"

"Nope," she found the energy to say, "I'll march right in and drag you out of the shower if you're not out in fifteen minutes after the game."

Pantier walked through the doorway and looked back over his shoulder. "I'd like that even better," he said, an eyebrow climbing.

"Out!" She laughed and threw the referee's shirt at the closing door.

Elaine leaned back against the long examination table. The cold metal rail supported her, and she took several deep breaths in an attempt to quiet her pounding heart. She toyed with the referee's whistle, feeling more alive and happy than she could remember ever having been. Every nerve in her body tingled keenly.

"Hey, Doc, we're on!" Phil Walters's voice pierced through the electric silence in the room and brought her back to reality.

"I'm coming," she shouted back. After gathering up the referee's shirt, she stuffed it and the whistle into her gym bag, grabbed her med kit, and ran out on unsteady legs to meet the others.

More than anything else Elaine had always liked the short pregame ceremony. As she stood with Cap at the end of the Hawks' player line, waiting to enter the arena, she listened to the rink announcer set up the crowd for their appearance.

*"And now, the Omaha Ice Palace asks you to welcome*

*the 1984 Stanley Cup champions and parent affiliate of the Hawks . . . the Edmonton Oilers."*

Appreciative applause filled the air as the announcer paused for the Oilers to skate onto the ice from the opposite side of the rink.

As the Oilers took their seats on the visiting team bench, the organist belted out the opening bars of "Chariots of Fire," the Hawks' theme song, and the crowd rose to its feet and began to roar. *"And, now, returning to the Ice Palace, for their twenty-fourth consecutive season, your very own Adams Cup champions."* He paused again and then shouted, *"The Omaha H . . . A . . . W . . . K . . . S!"*

With a standing ovation, some 6,000 fans greeted *their* hockey team. The Hawks, magnificently clad in black and gold, flashed onto the freshly glazed ice and streaked around the perimeter of the rink for a single, welcoming gesture to their adoring audience. Edmonton might be the big-leaguers, but the hometown team was showered with all the affection and attention its fans could muster. The Hawks were back on home ice.

The show lap ended, and three players stopped to offer their arms to the coach and Elaine and assisted them across the rink to the Hawks' bench. From the corner of her eye Elaine saw Phil Walters climbing to his vantage point near the press box, where he would watch the action and relay his observations by radio to Cap.

While she climbed the low risers behind the players to her place in the back row, Elaine also spied Roland. He was sitting next to the alternate goalie, grinning broadly. She sat down and looked over at him again; his thumbs-up signal told her that his spirits were up and that he fully approved of the Hawks' thousandfold fan club, which still continued its robust clamor.

As they all stood for the national anthem, she was able to get a reply across to him. It began as a victory sign but ended with her fingers crossed. He laughed, and they both turned their attention to Erwin Poppy, at his Mighty Wurlitzer, as he played and sang "The Star-Spangled Banner."

"Erwin will never replace Kate Smith," Paul Rutledge whispered to Elaine as the anthem finished and they sat down to watch the face-off.

"No." She laughed. "But he keeps trying."

Her mind tried to switch to automatic pilot as the action began. She'd done it time and time before, but Roland's presence seemed to short-circuit all natural brain function. Elaine had always had the ability to watch the game, alert for player injuries but still not totally wrapped up in the match. But that evening she could barely concentrate on more than the sideline activity.

Cap had always said that coaches and trainers should be cool, even aloof from the rough-and-tumble action if they really wanted to be effective. Still, tonight thoughts of Roland, not the game, rambled through Elaine's mind at an ever-quickening speed. Only the first-period break interrupted her daydreams.

The first period of play had been disastrous. The Hawks were sluggish, and they seemed disoriented by the highly skilled Oilers. The locker-room sermon that Cap presented during the first-period break was pure fire and brimstone at its best.

Elaine busied herself with rewrapping a player's ankle, but even she was drawn into the coach's spiel. He was working on them now. They just weren't giving it all that they had.

"I want you to *skate*. Hard. And don't give that puck away again," he said at the finish. With cigar dangling from his mouth, the coach marched back to his office, and they went at it for the second period.

The game improved: a loss of 3 to 7, but not bad at all for a batch of rookies. Still, Elaine had seen that the coach's speech had less direct effect than Pantier's sideline kibitzing. For the next two periods he hardly sat down. Oblivious to the action on the ice, she watched his every move.

Propped with one knee against the rail, he shouted a nonstop stream of commands to the players on the ice. Red-faced and sweating, he seemed to have lost touch with everything save the game, and Elaine was fascinated as she watched him play right along with the team from the bench.

The great black Panther pounded on the rail, paced back and forth, and conferred with Cap time and time again. Phil Walters blasted a persistent barrage of observations through the radio headset, and among the three of them the Hawks received a heavy concentration of commands, countercommands, and seasoned strategy—all of it through Pantier.

"Rush those two wing positions this time," Roland urged the defensemen, preparing them for another line change. "Keep on 'em; don't let them shoot. Don't even let them get near the goal. You can do it. Now get in there." The action continued as five Hawks flew back to the bench, and the next line jumped over the rail and attacked the Oilers mid-ice.

"Good job, Rutledge," Elaine heard Roland praise the returning line. "You, too, Stolypovcyk. You're both getting some good shots in."

By the end of the period Rutledge had scored his first goal of the season, while Stolypovcyk had racked up his first two penalties. It all evened out, and each player had something to remember from that first game—Roland saw to it.

His enthusiasm never waned, and when she met him outside the dressing room after the game had ended, he was not yet back down to earth.

"Did you see how Hadly grabbed that pass and ran!" he said happily. "They all did a really good job, don't you think, Doc?"

She nodded and smiled. This was a side of him she hadn't

71

seen before: the player, who found excitement and joy through his sport. Pantier's eyes were wide and electric; he continued to recap the game all the way to Murphy's. His enthusiasm was contagious.

The restaurant was swarming with players and fans. The festive atmosphere included several newscasters and two photographers who swung through the crowd, interviewing players and prompting comments from the fans.

Roland kept his hand on Elaine's. "I don't want to lose you in this mob," he said as they entered the restaurant.

"You can't," she replied, but he didn't hear her over the noise.

She tried to move away when a reporter came up to talk with him. "I'm not into cameras," she had to shout. Roland smiled as the cameraman moved in for a close-up and refused to let go of her hand.

"Tell us, Roland, how's your scouting assignment coming along? Are you going to have the cream of the rookie crop signed in time to get some play in with Edmonton this season?" The newscaster held a microphone up to Pantier's mouth.

"Well, here's my assistant. Maybe you should ask her how our scouting program's progressing," Roland replied, pulling Elaine closer to him. "This is Elaine D'Arte, the Hawks' senior trainer, and she is working with me in evaluating the rookies."

Now the microphone was in her face. "Tell us, Miss D'Arte, what is your opinion of the scouting so far? Is Roland going to get the job done in time to make it back to Edmonton for the second half of the season?"

"No problem," she replied, not at all comfortable with his aggressive stance. "Before Thanksgiving, I should think, we'll have seen all we need of the rookies, and he should be back on pro ice!" Roland gave her a broad smile. Elaine realized she had nothing to base her observation on;

72

it really wasn't a subject for speculation. Still, she could tell it made Roland feel much better and let it go at that.

"I want you to meet the Edmonton right wing," Roland told Elaine. Taking her by the wrist, he wound them both through the crowd toward a player standing near the bar. "Elaine, this is Emil Tolen. Emil, this is Elaine D'Arte, the Hawks' senior trainer."

The younger man smiled and slapped Roland on the shoulder good-naturedly. "And we've all been so worried about you, Pantier." He laughed. "Lost in the Nebraska wilderness, all alone!" Tolen shook Elaine's extended hand and punched Roland's arm. "It's nice to see you're not stranded in the minor leagues without company!" He winked at Roland, who showed barely a glimmer of approval.

And so he shuttled her from player to player. As soon as the introductions were completed, Roland's conversation returned to the normal course.

"I had trouble getting around that young Hawk goalie of yours," said an Oiler to Roland. "He's really sharp!"

Pantier grinned. "I told him all about your tactics, Hubert," Roland replied. "He was ready for you tonight!"

"Yes, but he was the only one," another Oiler chimed in. "Where did you get that batch of rookies anyway?"

"From Edmonton, where else?" Roland replied with a smirk, and the debate began in earnest.

Less than an hour after they had arrived, Roland was already taking in the latest news from Edmonton, cursing and discussing officials, and replaying the exhibition game with his mates.

Another two hours passed, and although Elaine enjoyed the enthusiastic commentaries, she grew restless. It was difficult to concentrate on anything but Roland. She wished they could be alone, that the crowd would just disappear and Roland would be left only to her.

He remained close to her but not close enough. He constantly touched her but not as she wanted to be touched. Elaine knew there could be more than a friendly squeeze of her arm or a momentary brushing of her shoulder. And she wanted it; she wanted more of him.

Finally, she decided it was best to withdraw from the frustration for a while and excused herself diplomatically from the group. Seeing Meg alone at a corner table, Elaine walked over and collapsed in a chair next to her friend.

"Look, Elaine, you're on the late news." Meg was watching a television set over the bar, and sure enough, there stood Elaine being interviewed. It was too noisy to hear how she sounded, but she looked fairly poised.

"First time I've been on TV in a long time," she said to Meggan. "Not bad at all."

"Well, if you keep hanging around superstars, it won't be the last! So, are you still going to tell me that there's nothing between you and Pantier?"

"No, I won't try that again." Elaine laughed. "We've gotten to know each other better this last week. He's not such a tough cat."

A waitress came over, and Elaine ordered a sandwich.

"Aren't you going to wait and eat with Roland?" Meg queried, ordering also.

"If I waited until he was ready, I'd starve."

She watched him for the rest of the night, relaxed and happy, home again with his mates, as he called them. Elaine was glad she'd given him an extra charge of optimism by leading the newsman to believe Edmonton would be recalling him. A small something perhaps, but she was happy to do it. After all, just knowing him had made her happy. It was a fair exchange.

He had dropped the macho act she deplored, and Elaine could see a very pleasing, subtle difference in Pantier that evening. He was careful to include the rookies at the table where most of the Edmonton players finally settled. Introductions were made, and the younger men were obviously

74

impressed at being considered equals of the seasoned Oilers.

Their conversation turned from generalities to specific criticism, but Pantier carefully guided the Oiler comments, and everyone was appeased: The Edmonton players had an opportunity to coach the rookies, and the rookies accepted it all graciously. Roland was a natural diplomat, and Elaine couldn't help admiring him for it.

She remembered his first appearance at Murphy's and how she'd judged him from that experience. As Meg talked at her, Elaine tried to overhear all that Pantier was now saying. She was glad to have given him the benefit of the doubt. He was much more real to her now than he had been in the beginning.

The crowd broke up by midnight. The players were not expected back for practice until Monday, but they had been told to report for a team meeting the next afternoon. Elaine had to check in as well and appreciated Roland's suggestion that they go on, too.

"Well, what did you think of them?" he asked as they returned to the complex.

"Nice, relatively normal—for hockey players, that is." She snickered so that he could see she was teasing.

"They're really a great bunch of friends," he said, stretching his legs and leaning back in the seat. "I've played with most of them for the past six seasons." There was a wistful quality to his voice, and she noticed that he stared beyond the windshield at nothingness.

"You miss them, don't you?" Elaine ventured.

"Not as much as playing," he replied. "Did you really mean what you told that reporter? About my getting back to Edmonton by Thanksgiving?"

"Did you really mean to say that I was part of your scouting party?" she asked in reply, trying not to complicate the situation by magnifying his hopes. Pantier just grinned at her, so she added, "I thought you'd prefer my being optimistic, especially in front of the media." Without pretense, she said it to him straight.

"At least you're thinking more like me lately, Doc." She'd stopped in front of his apartment, and he was about to get out. "And you're right, I did appreciate your being optimistic with that reporter. I don't need any bad press or foggy rumors starting up." His eyes looked tired. "My mates think you're pretty special," he added with a wink.

"Oh, it's just the shock of meeting a female trainer; they'll get over it." Now *she* was trying to prolong their conversation as they sat in her car. Surely he would kiss her again. Just once, she hoped.

"Well, there aren't many women in our business, that's for sure." He yawned. Neither of them spoke for a very long time.

"Remember when I asked you to show the team how you got to be a superstar?" Elaine finally asked him.

"How can I forget it?" He chuckled. "You said it right after you had shouted at me about making them into goons."

Elaine smiled. "Well, tonight really showed them what you're all about, Roland. Did you see how they responded to your sideline coaching?"

"I'm glad you saw it, too," he answered. "I thought it might just have been my imagination."

"Oh, I *saw* it. Those young men really hustle for you. I wouldn't say this to Cap," she said thoughtfully, "but the Hawks really have learned a lot from having you around. And I want to thank you for giving them your best."

Pantier produced a small grin and looked over at her.

"From someone who also gives them her best, I take that as a real compliment." His eyes never shifted from hers as he reached over and began to stroke her cheek with his hand. "Tell me," he asked, "why is it that we always give our very best away to someone else?"

"I—I don't follow you," Elaine replied, but she hadn't missed his meaning.

"It's something I've come to notice. Athletes do it all the time. The best that's in them is always given away. They give it to their teams, to the owners, the fans. It's as if they can't help themselves. We're a compulsive lot, don't you think? Whole careers spent in giving ourselves away. And then, when we can no longer play, we have nothing left to give back to ourselves."

"Occupational hazard," Elaine murmured. His words were simple, yet painfully true. The warmth of his hand only emphasized the depth Roland had touched in her.

"Not a hazard," he replied, opening the car door and getting out. "It's unavoidable and usually terminal."

Having thanked her for the evening, Pantier simply walked away without giving her the kiss she'd hoped for all evening long. A sudden emptiness clutched at her.

Elaine had trouble sleeping that night. Nothing bothered her, but the excitement of the evening and Roland's warmth gave her imagination a great deal to work with as the night moved on. *He* was special, she thought. Very, very special.

And when Elaine finally fell asleep, the referee's shirt was tucked beneath her arm.

# CHAPTER FIVE

"We've got a lot of work to do here," Coach Holloway continued. "I want a *team* out there on the ice—not a bunch of prima donnas doin' their own thing. Got that?" Everyone nodded automatically at the coach's command.

Since two o'clock he had been demonstrating that his photographic memory was still intact. For two hours he'd been playing tapes of the previous night's exhibition game, but only after he himself had drawn every moment of play from his memory. It was all fairly standard for Cap. He had to shake them up before they'd settle down and really start working.

With particular effort Elaine paid attention to every word, even though she found her interest wandering to Roland. He sat a few feet away, never looking at anyone but the coach. She wondered if he was thinking about her. Then, just as quickly, she turned the thought off and tuned in to Holloway again.

"We have our first league games this next weekend. You're up against Salt Lake City for a two-game stint. It's on home ice, and I want Omaha to see that you really can play hockey. You disappointed them last night, but they're a forgiving bunch of fans. Probably didn't expect much from you against the Oilers. But they're expecting some real hockey from now on." He looked at each face before him and removed the unlit cigar from his mouth. "I don't want this city embarrassed again," he growled, and Elaine almost laughed. His "hometown" speech got better with every season. The rookies, in particular, were really impressed by his theatrical flare.

"So how does a trainer spend her last available Saturday night?" Roland asked when only he and Elaine were left to walk out of the arena after the meeting ended.

She sighed, thinking that it would be five and a half months before any of them would have a full weekend free —or even two days in a row for relaxation. It was one of the few things about hockey that she never had adjusted to: working full speed while others were spending peaceful weekends with family and friends.

"Oh, there's my hair to wash and laundry to do," she impishly answered him.

"You're joking. That rejection is older than both of us combined." Roland groaned. But then he slipped a free hand under Elaine's arm, and they stopped. "Seriously, Miss D'Arte—"

"I think you can call me Elaine now that we're officially coaching together." She felt energy and confidence rising, even though his approach and solid touch still caused a violently sensual reaction. She had come to enjoy it, more than he could know.

"Good. I like Elaine much better. So, Elaine, may I buy you dinner? After all, we have a lot to discuss. You know, the rookies and all." He winked at her, and Elaine's heart began to pound.

"Do you need another ride or just a tour guide this time?" She chuckled, not wanting him to sense just how excited the proposition had made her.

"Neither. I'd just enjoy spending the evening with you. And for your information, my car is out of the shop now."

She laughed, a nervous reaction to the fact that he was actually asking her out. Suddenly Elaine became unsure of herself and began walking to gain a moment to recoup.

Fortunately the unsteadiness passed as quickly as it had begun. When she acknowledged that a shred of fear had maneuvered its way back into her psyche, she stopped and looked the Panther straight in the eye. Now that he had finally taken the initiative, Elaine had to work at bridling her response.

"I really should be working on the changes in our airline schedule and hotel reservations tonight," she said truthfully. And then she added a ploy of her own. "I'd love to have dinner, but I want to be home early so I can get some of this"—she pointed to the list of travel details Holloway had dictated—"organized." *Don't be too anxious,* she cautioned herself mentally, praying he wouldn't withdraw the invitation.

"If it's an early evening you require, madame, then an early evening it shall be." His velvety eyes beamed at her, and once again he winked. "I'll give you an hour or so to get ready and pick you up around, say, seven? We don't want to lose out on the last shore leave for months."

"Home by nine?"

"Only if you promise me that you will *not* waste an evening in laundry!"

"Scout's honor." Elaine held up two fingers, and they parted.

All the way home she applauded her renewed courage, never once regretting having accepted his offer. Tonight she was not going to share Pantier with anyone else.

The closer she got to home, the more excited Elaine became. And as she hopped from her car, she was striding and thinking at full speed. A little less than an hour and a half to get ready. Her mind whirled with details of showers, makeup, and . . . something to wear. What would she wear?

Moments later, showered and wrapped in a floor-length velour robe, she rifled through her closet in anxious deliberation. Clothes, clothes, clothes, and absolutely nothing appropriate. She collapsed onto the bed and stared at the walk-in closet, crowded with warm-up suits, skate gear, and extra uniforms. Where had her mind been for the past two years?

Two years. The time reference finally hit her. It had been more than two years since she'd really been out, and in that time her wardrobe had been diminished totally to casual, nondescript sportswear. Maybe he was taking her back to Murphy's, she thought with some relief. That was a casual place. No. She couldn't take the chance of his taking her, dressed as if she'd just come from the spa, to a more conventional restaurant. No. She wanted to wear something special, different for him.

Attacking with a vengeance, Elaine finally discovered a rose-colored sweater dress, hidden with a few other dresses and suits in the farthest recess of the closet. Perfect, not too dressy and not at all casual. She pulled it on and walked slowly toward the mirror.

The dress brought back happy memories, and she delighted in the way it still looked and fitted. The bodice was accented with pearl-centered hand-crocheted roses, and though snug, it attractively outlined the fullness of her bust and swept gracefully down and over the swell of her well-formed hips and thighs. Elaine now saw the dress, a favorite of hers, in a new light. It made her feel feminine in a way that she had not for a very long time.

She let a lighthearted anticipation gently seize her as she added pearl earrings, found a pair of open-toed mauve-colored heels to match the dress, and sat down in front of the mirror.

She brushed out her curly, shoulder-length hair into full peaks of dark honey, and she added a few combs to pull it slightly away from her face. She added a touch of mascara to already thick lashes and completed her efforts with a quick whisk of blush and lip gloss. With a long, appraising look, even Elaine was pleased at the transformation made in little more than an hour.

Just as she finished, there was a knock at the front door.

After rushing into the living room, Elaine discovered that Pantier had arrived early when she flung open the door.

He stood before her silently, not offering to move across the threshold. His large eyes, wide with undisguised approval, floated down her body with brazen familiarity, and Elaine found herself almost paralyzed beneath his seductive gaze.

"You're early." Elaine eventually found her voice. "Won't you come in?"

He walked in slowly and began to look around the room. "My watch must be fast," he replied casually. "You're an antiques collector?"

"Oh, a few pieces here and there. I'm not really a collector."

The shift in conversation put her back at ease, and she offered Roland a seat and a drink.

"A little wine would be fine," he replied, not settling in one spot but examining the old rocker by the window.

"Rosé or Chablis?" she called from the kitchen.

"Doesn't matter. Whatever you're having."

She peered back into the living room and saw that he was moving slowly from one end of the room to the other, engrossed in the odd assortment of furniture and collectibles she had gathered over the years.

Still reeling from the excitement of his unspoken compliment, Elaine struggled to uncork a bottle of Chablis, but finally gave up in exasperation as Pantier strolled into the kitchen.

"Your home is lovely, Elaine. May I help?" he asked, noticing her predicament. "I'm rather experienced at this."

He took the corkscrew from her hand and turned to the

counter. It was only then that Elaine had a chance to notice that he'd dressed in a trendy three-piece suit but was not wearing a tie. His shirt, with several buttons left undone, exposed his tanned dark chest, sprinkled lightly with silver gray.

She was tempted to touch him, to run her hands over his inviting skin. Instead, Elaine focused her attention on finding two wineglasses. Turned to a cabinet, her back to Pantier, she took a deep breath, held it, and counted to ten —slowly.

The concentrated effort paid off. Her trembling legs grew steadier, and her mind returned from its fantasy.

"Ah, here we go," he commented as she heard the cork release.

They took both glasses and the wine bottle back into the living room. But still he didn't sit down. With drink in hand, he paced in long, graceful strides from object to object, asking questions and looking rather shy and awkward.

Elaine found herself relaxing. The wine helped take the edge from her less noble thoughts, and his knowledge of antiques made her that much more determined to make their evening amicable.

"I love antiques, too," he added while helping Elaine into her coat. "There's not much time for bargain hunting during season, but I spend a great deal of my summers driving around the countryside, looking for unusual pieces that I can pick up for a song." They walked to his car, and he helped her in.

Although she found the conversation delightful, Roland's driving left much to be desired. As they rounded yet another corner at breakneck speed, Elaine interrupted just long enough to suggest he slow down.

"This isn't the Canadian countryside, Roland." Elaine noticed they were approaching an entrance to the interstate and shuddered to think how he would take it. "I would like to live a nice long life, and would appreciate every opportunity to do so." At her request he slowed down to a reasonable speed and entered the freeway traffic flow with little difficulty.

"I would have thought you'd love speed," he said, unperturbed by her caution. "Most skaters are thrilled by speed."

"Only French Canadians." She chuckled in an attempt to retrieve her humor. "They all try to be as fast off the ice as they are on!"

"Oh, madame, how you have wounded me," he said, shifting to a feigned French accent, complete with theatrical hand-to-chest gesture, just to prove how seriously he was wounded. Then, glancing at her smirking, unsympathetic grin, he added, "How heartless you are."

"You'll get over it, I'm sure," she said with a hint of a giggle. The thundering laughter that greeted her comment made her break into a laugh as well.

Torontino's was a favorite Italian restaurant of Elaine's, and when Pantier pulled into the parking lot, she was delighted by his choice.

"Oh, you'll love this place," she chattered as they walked around the corner and entered the two-story frame building. Warm, spicy smells hung in the air, waiting to be identified. "They make their own breads, you know," Elaine added, recognizing the fresh scent of hot yeast. "And all their own pastas."

"I know," replied Pantier as the hostess showed them to a small table in the main dining room. "Phil's told me all about it. I guess you two come here often."

Elaine blushed. Had Phil Walters led Pantier to believe they were lovers?

"You and Phil are very close, yes?"

"Well, we've worked together for the past couple of seasons." Elaine could hear the defensive tone in her own voice as she stumbled to find a suitable explanation. "He's married, you know. I mean—"

"I know. He told me that you are very good friends." Pantier seemed to take great pleasure in having thrown her a curve. He sat grinning, with one finger toying at the edge of his mustache and mischief gleaming in his eyes.

"Well, then you understand that we all come here—as a group—once in a while." With that, Elaine took temporary refuge behind the menu.

Pantier loved to eat; his appetite honestly intrigued Elaine, who watched him meticulously consume a huge antipasto and half a dozen bread sticks before the main course arrived.

Their conversation remained light and undirected, but somewhere between soup and a huge order of lasagna, Elaine's curiosity got the best of her.

"You've really surprised me, you know," she said as she continued to munch at her antipasto. "Why would a Frenchman want to come to an Italian restaurant? I would have thought you'd be quite a culinary purist. Escargot, quiche, cheese, and wine with hard bread."

"My mother's Italian," he replied between attacks on the entrée. "She believed that growing boys should eat nutritious, hearty—"

"Italian food," Elaine interrupted with a chuckle.

"Correct. More Chianti?" Elaine shook her head no.

"My mother is a very strong-willed woman. It took her twenty years to reeducate my father—"

"He's French?"

"Completely," answered Pantier with a grin. "Anyway, they finally compromised. My mother insisted that we eat Italian food, and my father insisted we go into hockey—"

"You and your mother?" Elaine tried to say it with a straight face.

"No—'we' meaning my father and I," he replied before taking another bite and smiling at Elaine's light comeback.

"So here I am. A professional French hockey player who's addicted to pasta! Sad, isn't it?"

"I'm surprised you have any personal identity left after such a difficult home life." Even though she got the words out without laughing, Elaine couldn't maintain her dry composure. Her laughter was contagious; soon Pantier had joined her. They sat looking at each other, without the slightest attempt from either side of the table to control their amusement and ignoring stares from the other diners.

"So you became a hockey player to please your father. Parental pressure? I'll bet you really wanted to be something else, right? And you've been struggling all these years, living his dream, not yours." She meant to tease him, but Pantier became quite serious.

"Actually," he said, still smiling, but completely intent, "he and I have had the same dream all along. I can't remember a time when I didn't want to be in hockey. He is very proud of me, and I've always been glad to have had the chance to make our mutual dream come true."

His eyes were softer now, and his face radiated a candor that she hadn't seen before. Elaine felt as if they were sharing some very special secret.

He leaned across the table and flashed a wide smile. "Would you believe that my parents have driven hundreds of miles *just* to see me play?" he asked.

"Yes," she replied. "Would you believe that my mother still sends boxes of cookies for all the players at Christmas?" Pantier chuckled and leaned back in the chair to resume his dinner. "Is that why you're so anxious to get back to Edmonton?" she asked.

"Oh, that's part of it. My parents have been much too concerned with my being put out on a scouting assignment, and I guess it would relieve their anxiety if I were playing again. But that's not all that important." He pointed to the lasagna, then to Elaine's plate. "You've hardly touched your dinner. Here, try some of this; it's terrific." With that he eagerly piled a large portion of his dinner onto a clean salad plate and handed it to Elaine, against her protests.

"I've never missed the start of a season in eighteen years, and I don't like it. Simple as that. It's just not a good omen. I want to get back to Edmonton as quickly as I can and start playing hockey again, to ward off the evil spirits, so to speak. More lasagna?"

Elaine let the subject drop there; she understood his resistance to getting into the role of the Hawks' player coach. His "omen" could be an indication of the end to his career—something she knew he wasn't ready to accept.

"Tell me how you became a trainer," he asked her. "Could it be that your parents always wanted you to coach?" He chuckled and continued to eat.

"Coaching was never a serious consideration," she answered, but she felt uneasy with his question. Elaine didn't know Pantier that well. Her own story seemed very inappropriate, considering how wrapped up he was in the fear of not being able to play professionally again. Instead of lying, she decided it was better to circumvent the truth—for his sake. "I've always loved athletics. My parents had me on skates by the time I was three." She stopped to take a bite of her salad and to think about her approach to the "truth."

"You're from Omaha then?" His question gave her still another minute to design her tale.

"No. From Boston originally. My family's still there."

"Then how did you come to be out here on the prairie?"

"Luck. Pure good luck." She giggled. "When I couldn't make the Olympic figure skating team . . ." Pantier laughed, not realizing that she had told the truth and thinking she was still teasing him. Elaine was oddly relieved that he hadn't taken her seriously, and she continued with confidence. "I enrolled in college, studied physical therapy, got certified in sports medicine, and came looking for the Hawks!"

"You're joking!" he cried. "Who in her right mind would actually go looking for a minor-league team like the Hawks?"

This time his laughter annoyed her. Her years with the Hawks had been very special; most of her happiest memories revolved around the team and her life in the prairie city.

"I did," she answered rather defiantly. "And I'm glad that I found them." Her eyes told Pantier that he'd misjudged the depth of commitment Elaine felt toward the team.

"I'm sorry," he said sincerely. "I guess I feel that way about Edmonton, too. But you have other options," he went on quietly.

"Oh?" Elaine smiled.

"Yes, the Sports Medicine Center," he said. "It could really use someone with your expertise."

"No comment" was all Elaine would say.

They finished dinner talking about the rookies and *their* problems, and as they walked to Elaine's front door promptly at nine, as he'd promised, she realized just how much she'd enjoyed their evening together.

"I'd invite you in for a nightcap," she explained as the front door swung open, "but I really do have to get some of these travel changes organized this evening."

"But no laundry, agreed?" Pantier replied lightly.

"No laundry. Thank you, Roland. It was a lovely evening. I really had a nice time," she said. But the words came out less enthusiastically than she had meant them to.

"It was my pleasure," he answered, leaning conspicuously against the doorframe with little sign of wanting to leave.

Suddenly Elaine was caught in the penetrating light of his eyes. She could think of nothing to say, and her heart began to race as he moved closer and reached out to place his hands on her shoulders.

Gently he pulled her to him, and she accepted his kiss. Her hands instinctively stretched upward and found the soft expanse of his chest through his open coat. Long, slender fingers kneaded the hot flesh; they moved beyond her control. His kiss was slow, reserved, not at all as she had expected it to be.

He kissed her again, holding her closer now and tasting her lips with his tongue this time. Elaine's heart pounded against his body; every fiber of her being screamed out to him, and she felt time itself stop. Only the taste of him and the power of their embrace mattered, and her mind recorded every second of sensation. Elaine desperately wanted him to kiss her harder, to hold her tighter, to offer her a release for the desire that once again threatened to consume her. All evening she had watched him, been near him, and struggled to maintain her composure.

Now there seemed no reason at all for her to be denied. Excited but unsure, she hesitated to encourage him, and instead of inviting *her* to share more of him, Roland lifted his head and looked into Elaine's eyes. She felt him release her. He offered her no choice, and she stepped back from him.

"You're beautiful, Elaine," he whispered, but she did not look up. Taking her chin with one hand, he tilted her head, and she was forced to look at him. "Beautiful, through and through."

Kissing her forehead, he turned to leave but stopped just outside the door. "Good night."

"Good night," she murmured with a faint smile.

Pantier closed the door, and she stood silently in the dark. With eyes closed, Elaine concentrated on the delicious urgency that rippled through her body, while savoring the last hint of his cologne.

"It's seven A.M., Omaha! Do you know where *your* morning paper is?"

"Under, on, or in between the shrubs—just where it always is." Elaine mumbled in reply to the radio announcer's cheerful sign-on message.

Radio WOW had just changed DJs for the second time since she'd tuned in at nine thirty the night before. Lying in bed, curled beneath a quilt, Elaine watched the first daubs of light flicker into the room. She could recall much of the station's late-night programming; except for a few hours, just before dawn, she'd listened to it all.

Sleep had thoroughly evaded her. She hadn't *felt* like sleeping. Her mind was far too busy for anything so mundane. Roland, and only Roland, had held her attention through the long night.

She'd felt confused and dismayed after he had left her. Sitting quietly alone in the dark living room, Elaine had wondered why he'd seemed so distant. Hadn't he realized how hopelessly excited she was; surely he had felt her tremble under his hands. Of course, he had!

Anger. Elaine spent the hours before midnight angrily denouncing him for toying with her: for all his sexy come-ons, for enticing and then leaving her with just a kiss, for all the buildup and, then, a frustrating "good night"! For all that, and more, she was angry.

As she tossed dishes into the kitchen sink and flailed soapy water in all directions, Elaine admitted that she had wanted him. The flurry of desire he'd left unsatisfied found its only release through several hours of continuous movement and aimless cleaning of the apartment.

The surge of physical energy had left her drained at last, and finally, she had crawled into bed, turned on the radio, and continued to brood about Pantier.

Just when or how the other possibility had occurred to her, she couldn't remember. But as she lay in the morning sunshine, Elaine laughed at herself for being so hotheaded and unreasonable.

His kiss, the whole evening had been too warm and genuine. It was not a ploy; Roland had not been toying with her emotions. She remembered the expression on his face as he left. He had been struggling with himself, holding back. Holding back. His motive was much more honorable than she'd given him credit for, and in the early, early hours Elaine concluded that they had tested each other, honorably tested to see if the attraction between them was real and compelling.

The radio still hummed in the background as she took one last turn beneath the quilt and stretched lazily. It felt very good just to be awake, thinking and remembering.

His face appeared each time she closed her eyes, and if she concentrated just a little, Elaine swore that she could hear his laughter and feel the firmness of his body next to hers. She shut her eyes one last time and waited for the heady flutter of excitement that insisted on accompanying any thought of the dark French Panther.

She'd felt so alive, so alert that she hadn't wanted to sleep after the pleasant realization. Afraid that the sensation could be diluted by sleep or maybe just wanting to experience it, deeply, without interruption, Elaine had spent a wakeful, fantasy-filled night. He had wanted her, too. A chivalrous Frenchman! Pantier had been just as unsure as she. At least he'd had the courage to ask. That was it —his kiss had been a question.

The reasoning didn't really matter, she thought. Only the excitement and the possibilities concerned her that late fall morning.

Unbundling herself from the quilt, Elaine found her robe and slippers, trotted to the front door, opened it, and began searching for the newspaper.

The air, clear and sharp, greeted her briskly, and she

stopped to take a long, slow breath before walking back into the house. Even the air seemed different somehow.

A few cups of coffee later Elaine had barely looked at the paper. Even the sports section didn't hold her interest. Instead, she paced from one window to another, surveying the morning and marginally trying to organize her day into something reasonably constructive.

*Just too much energy,* she thought as she aimlessly moved plants from window to window, and pounded the sofa cushions a second time. She had to get her unnatural high under control.

Thoughts of Pantier held her spellbound. She wanted to be with him again. If nothing else, being near him was all she wanted. But how?

As she walked down the hall to her bedroom, it came to her. She'd seen him out on morning jogs before. Maybe . . .

In a flash she changed into a pink cotton warm-up suit and laced up her jogging shoes. Pulling a knitted cap down over her ears, Elaine flew out into the frosty morning, still struggling with her gloves.

Twelve blocks to a mile, she reminded herself of the familiar rule of thumb. Down her own street, around the corner, and into a long, straight block of neatly landscaped brick houses, she jogged at a steady pace, feeling the air move around her and the intense energy within her releasing itself steadily. As she ran, she watched closely for Pantier.

Enjoying the rush of air and the peace within, she ran the first ten blocks with ease, turned onto another street, and began to double back over a course she had plotted long before. Having left the street, she jogged down a bike path and through the woods. Trees, barren after a single week of cold rain, rattled above her; the path, deep in brittle leaves, crunched noisily beneath her feet.

Another mile passed, and she began to tire. Her pace

slowed, and she held out her arms—a gesture of the freedom and unnamed joy that had suddenly appeared inside her.

At the edge of the wood she stopped running and jogged in place to a slower rhythm. Perhaps she would find him on the return route. Taking deep breaths and resting, she didn't notice the crunching approach of another runner until she turned to retrace the path.

It was Pantier, dressed in hockey shorts and a sweat shirt, approaching at a moderate run. Just seeing him made her heart rate climb once more. Lithe muscles, expanded from running and well defined in the morning sun, extended evenly up his legs. Muscular arms worked steadily from his sides and swung in cadence to his step.

Though not as graceful a runner as he was on ice, he still had power and agility. Waving, Elaine began running toward him.

"What brings you out so early?" she asked innocently as they met and stopped to jog in place.

"This is Phil's idea of weekend endurance testing." He panted. "I tried to tell him I wasn't a football player, but he wouldn't listen. I've been assigned two miles a day for the next week. Where's the one-mile marker?"

"You overshot it about a mile back." She laughed. "Come on, I'll walk back with you."

"God bless you," he answered, still panting hard, as they turned and walked back through the woods and onto the lawn behind Elaine's condo.

"Do you have time for a cup of coffee?" she asked, not wanting to appear too forward but not wanting him to leave either.

"Only if it's good and hot. I'm freezing."

She brewed a fresh pot of coffee and teased him, saying he should be wearing more appropriate clothing. Then she disappeared into the bedroom and returned to hand him a quilt. He wrapped it around his legs and sat back down at the kitchen table, still shivering.

"You should be more like me," she said teasingly. "See? If you dress right, you'll enjoy it more. The cold won't get to you at all."

"Is that so?" One eyebrow shot up, and his mustache curled around a menacing grin. "Then why do you still have your cap on?"

Elaine flushed, then laughed and pulled the hat off. Pantier laughed, too, as she tossed the cap on top of the refrigerator.

"How about some breakfast? Or have you eaten already?" she asked with hope that he'd accept. And he did.

"I see you've made great progress on the travel schedule," Pantier commented while she was busy assembling scrambled eggs, bacon, and toast.

The airline flight book, her notes, and Cap's itinerary still lay, undisturbed, on the table from the night before.

"I couldn't get into it last night," she said honestly. "But I'm planning to plow through it today."

He picked up the bulky schedule book and moved her clipboard to his side of the table. Without further comment, he started digging into the book and making notes. Elaine tried to concentrate on breakfast, while he grumbled about timetables and layovers.

"Do you know how many flight changes there are between here and Birmingham?" he finally asked. "Three. Can you imagine that? Three different planes to go eleven hundred miles."

"Is it any better between Edmonton and St. Louis?" she asked, referring to his regular travel schedule with the National Hockey League.

"No. And there's no excuse for it! How can players be expected to perform at peak efficiency when they're worn out from just getting to the games? Remarkable."

She stirred the eggs and said she couldn't agree more.

NHL or International Hockey League, majors or minors—it made no difference. Away-from-home games put the players under a lot of needless stress and strain.

"And the hotels," she added, serving their breakfast. "They're just as bad."

"Uh-huh," he answered. Laying the schedule and clipboard aside, Pantier said, "I never can sleep away from home. Hotels are noisy. Do you have any catsup?"

Elaine made a face but found the catsup. He was going to put it on his eggs. Catsup on eggs—he was *so* Canadian.

"You should try it." He encouraged her by handing back the bottle. "Really enhances the flavor."

"I'll pass, thank you."

They ate and continued to talk about the itinerary. But when they finished breakfast, Roland made no effort to leave. Instead, he offered to help her work out the details. Pleased that he wanted to stay, she made more coffee, and they started to work on the travel schedule together.

Just before noon the phone rang. It was Meg.

"Hi, you're up. Have to talk to you. Won't take a minute." She didn't wait for an answer, and Elaine barely had time to hang up before all 123 pounds of bubbling Meggan came bounding through the unlocked front door.

"I have this wonderful idea, Elaine. That is, it *will* be wonderful if you'll just help me out." Meg had got as far as the kitchen door and was about to explode in a second wave of chatter when she caught sight of Pantier, still sitting at the table, wrapped in a bright postage-stamp quilt.

Unaffected, as only Meg could be, she gave Elaine a coy pinch on the arm and sat down at the table. "Well, this *is* a very pleasant and auspicious surprise. I really wanted to talk to both of you!" The comment sounded good, if illogical. Still, none of them seemed to notice.

"So what's the problem?" Pantier replied with equal verve. He pushed away the airline book and gave Meg his complete attention. Elaine, still in shock, walked to the counter and poured another cup of coffee just to gain a momentary delay in the action. Pantier and Meg exchanged belated "good mornings," while Elaine tried to pull her blood pressure back down to normal.

"Well, I hope you two aren't doing anything this evening." Meg began again, but more slowly this time. "You see, I'm having a small dinner party, just four of us, and I need—I mean, you two are invited."

"That's half the party," said Pantier with a straight face. "Who'll make it a foursome?" Elaine caught the twinkle in his eye and relaxed even more. He didn't seem the least bit embarrassed or upset by either Meg's invasion or her invitation.

"Actually I haven't asked him yet. But you know the new rookie Joe Stolypovcyk?"

Elaine and Roland exchanged a quick, knowing glance. Both of them knew exactly whom she was referring to. At six feet four inches, the shy rookie from Cleveland had become infamous in just a few short weeks. What he lacked in style, Stolypovcyk made up for in unadulterated enthusiasm and drive. Elaine wondered if the bashful young man was really ready for Meg.

"Well, we had dinner together at Murphy's the other night, and I wanted to repay him with a nice home-cooked dinner this evening." Her vim was fading slightly as she saw Elaine and Pantier trying to hide wise smirks.

"Seriously, you two, he's a terrific guy but awfully shy. And I thought, well, if I invited two other people, he might not feel so uncomfortable."

It went without saying that Meggan had thought it through carefully. If the young player knew he was going to have dinner with Pantier, her evening would be set.

"That's why I was so glad to see you here, Roland," Meg went on. "We all can talk it over, just the three of us, and

96

then I'll call Joe. What do you say, huh? How could either one of you pass up an offer like that?"

Elaine and Roland looked at each other again, this time with Elaine trying not to show any real enthusiasm. Even though she felt very much like Meg at that moment, she didn't want Pantier, or Meggan for that fact, to know.

"What's the menu?" Pantier asked immediately. Meg rattled off an unabridged version of the index to her Greek cookbook.

"I don't know any Polish dishes. Greek's close enough, don't you think?" she asked.

"Definitely," replied Elaine. "Less than two thousand miles. Why not?"

"Roland?" Meg's eyes pleaded for an affirmative answer, and he supplied one.

"Only on one condition, however: I bring the wine."

His comment boosted Meg's enthusiasm. She started to leave without even asking for Elaine's acceptance. "That's seven tonight. I live just across the courtyard—"

"I know," said Elaine.

"Right," Meg answered, heading for the front door. "And by the way, don't worry about having to stay late. I wouldn't mind at all if you just popped in, ate, and popped right out again. You two might like to catch a nine o'clock movie or something. See you later." And she was gone.

As soon as the door closed, Elaine began to laugh. Roland stood up, removed his quilt, and handed it to her with a flair.

"I guess we're on an early schedule again this evening," he said nonchalantly. "I wish the airlines ran on the same schedule as the Omaha Hawks' social agenda."

They walked to the door, and Roland gave her a quick kiss. "I'm off to prepare for our gala evening at Meg's," he said, taking his hand from the doorknob and wrapping both arms around Elaine's waist. He hugged her tightly, and she responded without a moment's thought by weaving her arms under his and holding him close.

His scent was clean and pungent, and his legs were still warm from the quilt. Lowering his head, Roland rubbed his mouth along her cheekline and kissed her ear. His simple act aroused her instantly. But Elaine did not pull away. Rather, she held his body against hers and savored the delicious, impulsive thoughts that crackled in her head.

Unhurried and now certain that he felt it, too, she relaxed in his arms and smiled.

Their lips touched, and she quivered. For the first time Elaine noticed the feathery edge of his mustache as it brushed under her nose, and she chuckled.

"What is it?" he asked, withdrawing from their kiss and looking at her curiously.

"You have a mustache," she said with a giggle.

"You just noticed?"

"No, it just tickled me!" She looked into his great dark eyes and saw them narrow with thought.

"You'll grow to like it." He winked.

"I've grown to like you," she said boldly.

"I'm glad to know that."

His mouth fell hot and moist on her face. Slowly, artfully Pantier stroked the curve of her cheek with the tip of his tongue. As he returned to her lips and enticed them to open, Elaine closed her eyes and floated to the pulsing of her limbs. She became weightless in his embrace; her fingers lifted effortlessly to his face, and she held his mouth to hers.

Then she felt his head move away, and she opened her eyes to see Roland smiling down at her.

"Tonight," he whispered and kissed her forehead.

*Tonight,* she thought in reply.

## CHAPTER SIX

After finishing the itinerary, Elaine spent the rest of the lazy Sunday afternoon napping beneath the same heavy quilt that Roland had worn so regally in her kitchen. Wind rattled the windows of her bedroom, and she drifted in and out of cozy dreams for hours.

Her dreams were of Roland. She recapped the weeks from the first day they'd met. The foggy simplicity of her fantasies added subtle touches of courage rediscovered and rewards received. Had she allowed the dragon to consume her, Elaine might never have experienced the sheer joy and excitement Roland Pantier had brought into her life again.

Meg called late in the afternoon and roused Elaine from her dreams. She rushed in, borrowed something from the kitchen, and left.

With renewed energy after Meg had left, Elaine found herself gaining momentum. Showered and refreshed, she went through the ritual of deciding what to wear.

The choices were easier that night. A pair of nice jeans and a tailored silk blouse would be appropriate. She dressed with an approving eye on the mirror. The red blouse highlighted her dark hair. Open at the throat, long and belted over the jeans, it added a sensual, exotic quality to both her face and her form. She felt inviting in red, and she liked the soft, clinging texture against her body.

Then she put on a simple gold necklace and a pair of

small gold earrings. *Roland will like this,* she thought. Red silk and gold jewelry suited her mood perfectly.

His reaction was much the same as it had been the night before. Silent, approving, his eyes flickered with her image.

"Too much gold?" she asked, trying to tempt a comment from him.

"Not at all," he answered. "You're perfect." With a kiss he sealed it, and arm in arm, they walked across the courtyard to Meggan's.

As instructed by Meg, they arrived on time, and Elaine, at least, planned on leaving early. Meggan wanted Joe all to herself, just as Elaine wanted to be quietly alone with Roland. Little more about the evening really interested Elaine; she found herself watching the time, helping Meg expedite dinner, so they both could get on with more pressing plans.

To Elaine's delight, Roland cooperated completely. Although he seemed relaxed and interested from the predinner ritual right through dessert, Pantier began making departure provisions as soon as dinner was over.

"I felt a hundred years old," Roland said later as they sat watching the ten o'clock news in Elaine's living room.

"You sounded so wise and experienced in the ways of hockey, Roland. Even I was nearly overcome with reverence." Elaine batted her eyes and leaned toward him in mock fascination.

"Just call me Father Hockey," the Panther growled. "Damn, these young guys make me feel ancient at thirty-eight. They look at me like some wizened mentor that skates by magic!"

Although he'd played it straight with the rookie, doing his very best to keep the conversation an equal exchange between them, Elaine had watched a growing impatience in Pantier as Joe pressed him for tales of the "good old

100

days." She was pleased to see another, more realistic side of Roland as he humorously complained to her about it.

"I think we've done our part for Meggan's romantic scheme," Elaine said. "They *do* make a cute couple. Do you think Joe likes her?" It had been hard to tell who was the more nervous: Meg, hostess extraordinaire, as Roland called her, or Stolypovcyk, who hung on every word Pantier formed.

"Of course. He's not stupid. Shy maybe, but he's interested," Pantier replied as he took a sip of his drink and changed channels on the TV by remote control.

"How can you tell?" asked Elaine, wondering if the answer might give her additional clues to Roland's feelings about her.

"Well, for one thing he actually ate two servings of . . . what was it?"

"Stuffed grape leaves," Elaine answered.

"Okay. Stuffed grape leaves. And he didn't even ask what they were stuffed with. He just kept eating them." Elaine giggled at his reasoning. No one had had the nerve to ask, but only Stolypovcyk had eaten more than absolutely required.

Pantier moved closer to Elaine and slid his arm across the back of the sofa and behind her neck.

"And as another point of reference," Pantier went on, "Joe was wearing one of *my* best sweaters. Shows he really wanted to impress her."

"How did he get one of your sweaters?" Elaine asked, but she had lost interest in the conversation. As Pantier moved even closer to her, she felt a distinct heat enveloping her body.

"I would imagine," he replied, leaning over to whisper in her ear, "that my rookie roommate, the dashing Claude Vosienne, *requisitioned* it to help the poor boy out." Roland was purring again. Elaine felt the heat of his breath on her neck; the warm scent of his body permeated the room.

"Surely Vosienne wouldn't do that," she said, her mind no longer on the evening's gossip.

"Surely he won't be able to do it again once I've adjusted his thinking," he stated and moved his arm off the sofa to slide it across her shoulder. Elaine, expectant and smiling, let his other arm surround her waist and moved into the curve of his shoulder.

There was total silence as Elaine and Roland gazed into each other's eyes. The moment she'd prayed for had finally arrived. They were alone, comfortably wrapped together in seclusion. No prying eyes, no possible interruptions. Only the moment. Just the two of them.

The spell was cast, and Elaine thought she was prepared. Then her pulse began to race, and she suddenly felt giddy —unsure but helpless in the sweep of desire.

Would he only hold her, kiss her, and then depart? How could she bear another untimely separation? She was afraid: afraid she could not survive anything less than his loving her and afraid she might demand it if it were unoffered.

Emotion rose precariously within her, transmitting a dull, hungry ache to her very core. Elaine searched Roland's eyes for a clue to his intention. Quietly he kissed her forehead; his fingers tightened at her waist.

Was she mad? Her head began to swim with sudden, jarring confusion. What was she doing? Why? Was this what Pantier had wanted her for all along? Now she had willingly set the trap herself. Fear appeared once again, but this time Elaine saw the dragon approaching; she saw it before it struck at her.

Roland was smiling, totally unaware of the battle raging in her mind. She smiled, too, but from an inner resolution —a confirmation. No dragon of the mind would keep her from having love again. No unfounded fear would hold her back now.

Elaine kissed Roland's chin once more and nuzzled his smooth cheek with her nose. She had made up her mind.

Roland's chest expanded in a deep sigh. "Have you ever been kissed by an ancient hockey player?" he murmured.

"Never," she whispered in return and kissed his chin lightly. "Have you ever kissed your trainer?"

"Never."

One arm went around Elaine's shoulders. The other moved across her body to clasp both her legs. In a single powerful motion Roland lifted her onto his lap.

Elaine's arms slid around his strong neck and felt the thick, wavy hair along the nape. Her fingers curled up the sides of his head, and she gently nudged it closer.

His great dark eyes glimmered, and a half smile appeared. "You look like a Gypsy tonight, Elaine, the portrait of a Gypsy." Roland kissed her lightly, his eyes drawing in each detail of her face.

"I feel like a Gypsy," she answered in a voice that was husky and deep. Again she nudged his head with her palms, and his mouth met hers.

She traced his mouth, as he had traced hers the night before. From the fullness of his upper lip, across and down to the lower expanse, Elaine slowly, meticulously curved her tongue to match the changing surface of Roland's wide, lush mouth.

He quivered, and the sensation transported itself instantly through her arms and down, deep into her body. Elaine felt a rush of intense, sympathetic desire, like a pulsating wave of electric current as he gave in completely to her beckonings.

She felt his hard, large hands wind their way up her spine, replacing the cool texture of silk with tantalizing rivulets of heat from his fingers. As she continued to sample his mouth, it seemed as if his entire body had begun to glow white-hot. Elaine melted deeper into his embrace, her very spirit aflame.

Together they explored the damp, sweet recesses of each other's mouths. In great detail, with slow, purposeful moves, their tongues fenced back and forth, sparking embers of passion as they met.

His hand wandered from her back and descended to her hip. The heat transferring through the denim jeans and into her leg proclaimed his presence, and the light, kneading pressure of his hand as he found the softness of her inner thigh taunted her with devilish delight.

The buttons of his shirt gave way at Elaine's insistence, allowing her to move freely against the supple range of his upper body. As she kissed the edge of his ear, her hands spanned his chest, and her fingers crawled through the lush silvered fur.

"Lie back," he murmured in her ear. "Let me love you, my wonderful Work of Art."

As if in slow motion, they reclined in unison and sank into the thick cushions. He seemed suspended above her, somewhere in the shadows. Although she could no longer see his flashing eyes, his incandescent touch conveyed each artful move.

Elaine found the collar of his shirt and drew it back and away from his neck. It fell over his shoulders, and he helped her pull it down his arms and off. Carefully he unbuttoned her blouse, letting the front panels slide away.

Now kneeling above her, Roland bent to kiss her neck. With one hand cupping her head, he traveled along the slender outline of her throat and down the edge of her lace bra. His tongue flickered beneath the lacy cup and drew a wide, damp line into her cleavage, while his other hand deftly released the front clasp.

A low, languishing moan filled the silence, and Elaine arched as his tongue lapped hungrily at her erect nipple, then tugged gently to tease her even more, before moving to explore the other supple breast.

Once more she felt his feathery mustache, as his head

coursed down her body in slow, erotic motion. It floated across her abdomen, leaving a tingling wake of pure expectation when his tongue retraced the line.

She reached out and stroked his head; her fingers drew around his ears and combed through his thick hair. His spicy cologne mixed with the heat of their bodies to create a vivid illusion of faint incense in the air. It poured into her mind, and she felt intoxicated, almost giddy.

Being with him was more than Elaine could ever have imagined. Gentle, yielding, sensitive, the dark, sensuous Panther in her arms made her forget all inhibition and every memory she'd ever had of love. He stole the past and replaced it with promises for her tomorrows.

She felt him unfasten her jeans and ease them down her legs. He paused, somewhere near in the still darkness, and she heard a slight rustle. A second later he returned to her, and she felt his sleek, hot flesh slide along her body.

His desire, pronounced and smooth against her, incited Elaine to greater boldness, and she slid her hands along his torso, searching for the source of magnetism that charged between them.

It was as if there had never been another man in her arms before. All thought of the past vanished. Guiltless in her realization, Elaine accepted his every enticement and offered him every impulse that claimed her. In the stillness of the night, Elaine loved the man Pantier, and he loved her with every strength he possessed.

"Heaven help me, Elaine," he groaned as she stroked him. "I've got to have you. Please, please. Now."

"Yes, oh, yes," she answered.

No dragon of the mind could dissuade her. She wanted him, and nothing else at that moment meant more. What was there to fear? Any terror or confusion was tenderly subdued by his touch. The heat of his body protected her from doubt.

Pantier searched her body and discovered wants,

desires, and pleasures she had long forgotten, while he showed ways of loving her that she'd never known.

She was safe, secure in his arms, as protected as on the day he had danced with her on the ice. He held her before him—above his own need. Safe from the pain of anything less than perfection, Elaine yielded completely.

For what seemed an eternity that night, they savored the fire of passion. Flames rose and diminished between them, only to be reignited by a single touch or a quiet supplication.

Near dawn they fell into exhausted sleep within the pillows of the wide sofa. With his arms laced about her, her head resting in the shelter of his shoulder, they lay at peace with each other, sharing dreamy memories of a love finally discovered.

Someone was talking to her. A faint buzz of voices had infiltrated her sleep. Elaine tried to ignore it but to no avail. She started to turn over, but something held her in place. Opening her eyes, she focused on the window, brightly framed in sunshine.

Roland stirred; she looked over at the beautiful man beside her. His arms were wrapped around her; his head still rested on her breast. Elaine closed her eyes once more to concentrate on the steady rhythm of his breathing as he slept.

It hadn't been a dream, she mused. He had really made love to her all night long.

Elaine touched his hair. Yes, he was real, and he was in her arms.

Roland shifted again, his arm moved and tightened around her abdomen, and his legs stretched out alongside her body as they lay together on the deep, wide couch.

She nestled her chin on the top of his head. His soft, thick hair brushed across her face. Sound again. What was that awful buzzing that kept her from totally centering on this peaceful moment? Voices.

Still inebriated by hours of loving, Elaine struggled to make out the sound, to clear the haze of her sleepy mind.

She opened her eyes. Nothing seemed to fit. Where had she awakened? This wasn't her bedroom. And what was she on? Her body spanned the uneven sofa cushions. Living room. Yes, she was in her own living room, lying across two sections of the pit couch. Comforted by those few details, she closed her eyes again.

Then it hit her.

Morning. Monday morning. The radio alarm had gone off in the bedroom, and station WOW was broadcasting an hourly news update. But what *hour?*

She was startled by the realization that they had overslept. Work! Elaine's heart skipped. Her body jerked involuntarily, as if trying to jar her to full consciousness instantly. But when she tried to move, Roland held her only more tightly.

Time! What time was it?

She stretched to feel along the coffee table for her watch, while Roland sighed and began to mumble.

"Where are you going?" he whispered, his deep voice husky with sleep.

"I've got to find out what time it is," she answered, still palming the surface of the table for the watch.

He reached over and grabbed her arm just as she snatched the watch.

"I can tell you what time it is," he moaned in her ear and began kissing the side of Elaine's neck. His hand released her arm to begin a slow, feathery descent down her body. And as he stroked her inner thigh, Elaine dropped the watch on the floor and willingly flowed back into his embrace.

Their lovemaking superseded any other thought or

107

sound. The radio was no longer heard, replaced by the rapid, uneven chorus of their breathing.

An hour later they lay absorbed in each other, satisfied and spent, lavishly soaking up the sunshine that fell on them from the window.

"You're very late, you know." Elaine poked a finger at Roland's chest and sighed.

"You think so?" He yawned. "I thought I was right on time again."

Elaine giggled. "For your workout at the gym," she explained.

"No, thank you. I've had my workout for the morning."

He began to tickle her, and she began to wrestle his two-hundred-pound frame.

"It's useless to fight me, madame," he rasped. "I outweigh you by a hundred pounds or more."

"Leverage," she shouted, while trying to wiggle free. "Just a matter of leverage. Weight is immaterial."

"Oh." He smirked. Like lightning, he gently pinned her beneath him. Immobilized, she stopped struggling. "Give?" he asked, smiling down at her.

"I gave at the office!" she cried.

"That's a good idea," Roland said, thinking. "Your office, the kitchen—" Elaine caught him off-balance then and rolled him onto the floor. "And the floor. That's even better," he said and pulled her over on top of him.

"You're awful." She laughed. "Just awful."

"I know." He kissed her tenderly. "And I'm so good at it!"

Reluctantly they agreed that the day must begin. Still on the floor, they found her watch and lazily thought about their schedules. It was only ten o'clock. No harm done. Roland could skip one day at the gym, and Elaine wasn't due at the arena till one.

As if the rest of the world had dissolved into thin air, they lay on the living-room floor and talked.

"You shower first," she finally suggested. "And I'll fix breakfast."

He kissed her lightly and slapped her behind. "Right, chief!" he replied.

She was listening to him shower as she mixed omelets at the counter when a sobering fact crossed her mind. It crashed through her idyllic reverie, and Elaine stopped and rushed toward the bathroom. Roland, wrapped in a towel and dripping from head to foot, met her in the hallway.

They stared at each other; both of them had had the same thought.

"What are we going to do?" Elaine found the words first. "You can't go to practice in street clothes. And—"

She could tell that Roland was thinking only of the immediate problem of having to return to his apartment for his practice uniform. Then Elaine saw his face change; his eyes narrowed in more serious thought.

"Don't panic," he said quietly. "I'll think of something." They were silent again. The fear of being found out by the rest of the team was an unmentionable possibility that they both silently acknowledged. Elaine was much more vulnerable than Roland. Her professional status with the younger players was terribly important. Then there was Cap and his unbending code of conduct.

Roland put his arm around Elaine's bare shoulders. "And don't worry," he said, walking her back toward the kitchen. "I'm not about to have tongues wagging over us. This is our affair." He laughed at the double meaning of his own words, and Elaine smiled. He kissed her forehead. "We're not going to be headline news in Omaha tonight."

"Oh, God," Elaine gasped. "Meg. And Vosienne." Just the thought of Roland's roommate made her feel faintly sick. He'd know Roland had spent the night away.

Hastily, all too hastily she questioned having become involved with Pantier. He saw it in her eyes and moved closer to hold her. She squeezed him, but the panic did not subside.

"Are you sorry about us?" he asked.

"No." She wasn't worried; she was just afraid. "It's just that I value my privacy, that's all." They both realized how hard that was going to be to manage. The whole team lived within one huge condominium complex. For seven months a year they lived as a family unit: traveling together, training together, and sharing nearly every waking moment.

"We can end it now," he whispered. "If you want to, I'll understand. But just tell me *now.*"

She gazed into his eyes and saw that he meant it sincerely. "Is that what you want?" Elaine had to ask.

"No, but it's not my problem really." He was right. No one would think much of his having an affair. For a single man, for a superstar with celebrity privilege, nothing less would be expected.

Elaine, on the other hand, couldn't afford such luxuries. Her work and effectiveness depended solely on respect. She'd learned early in her career that to gain the team's confidence and esteem, she had to appear nearly perfect, almost superhuman. The players could never see her as a woman with emotions and needs. The warm, caring side of her could come only forward on a nonpersonal, thoroughly professional level: trainer to player, never one feeling human to another.

A visible relationship with Pantier would quickly undermine all she'd worked for. The other players would see her vulnerability, and her effectiveness would vanish, she was certain of it.

It had been different when Tony was alive. She suddenly recalled. He had been the Hawks' own superstar, with a certain status and respect that encompassed her work as well.

Bitterly she thought how unfair it all was. Without a protector, without marriage, she was supposed to fight her

110

normal instincts. Denying the affection and attention of another human being, she was expected to live a solitary life if she wanted to retain the years of professional respect she'd worked so hard to earn.

These problems had never surfaced before. Now, looking into Roland's face, Elaine realized she, too, deserved it all. She could accept nothing less.

"What are you thinking?" Pantier finally asked.

"That I want to live my own life."

Hugging her, Roland told her, "Then we'll work it out." Taking one problem at a time, they worked through what they could do about that day.

Because everyone was now scheduled for the morning workout at the gym, they felt certain that Roland could return to his apartment, gather up his gear, and never be confronted by Vosienne.

"He'll think I've been *occupied.*" Pantier chuckled.

"What about your car?" she asked.

"I walked over last night. Remember? Vosienne will think I prowl on foot."

It sounded weak, but they agreed that one night wasn't going to make a difference because no one yet had a reason to suspect their intimacy.

"I feel like a bank robber, plotting a heist." Elaine giggled.

"Not a heist," he told her. "That's tomorrow. Today we're planning alibis."

"And what about tomorrow?" Elaine wondered if it was really possible to keep from being discovered, even though she never once considered how many tomorrows there might be.

"First thing I get my own apartment. I can't stand having a roomie anyway," he said. "Trainers excluded." And he winked.

"You would actually do that for me?"

"If it means taking some of the pressure off you," he

answered. Having Vosienne so close to Roland was a major stumbling block to their plan. "Besides, I can well afford to pay for my own housing while I'm here, right?"

He made it sound so easy that Elaine agreed to the plan without a second thought. It seemed right, fair, and Pantier's honest concern melted away any doubt that arose.

"Now what about Meg?" he wanted to know.

"I'll keep the door locked!" Elaine promised. Meggan really wouldn't be a threat, she assured him. And knowing Meg as she did, Elaine felt confident that she would never say or do anything to harm her. "Meg's like a kid sister," she explained to Roland. "If she gets curious, she'll ask me."

"And then what will you do?"

Elaine was sure their secret would be safe with Meg. "I'll tell her the truth, Roland." Elaine knew she couldn't lie. That was completely beyond her. Concealing one's private life was acceptable; denying the truth of her life was unconscionable. There was nothing wrong with wanting Roland and having him in her life, although it might be misconstrued.

"Even if worse comes to worst, I'll never lie about us," she said. "I'm not ashamed."

"Neither am I." He smiled and held her hand. "I couldn't lie about wanting you, Elaine." He reminded her that it was privacy they both wanted to maintain, and she sensed a security in his words that removed any further worry.

From that moment on, their life together became a marvelous adventure. Their plottings provided suspense, excitement, and even intrigue. Somehow it all added to the splendor and fairy-tale quality of their relationship.

Secretive as they were, it never seemed to bother either of them. The gamelike quality only made the loving better.

Roland requested and received another apartment assignment; it was one of six efficiencies that the Hawks used

112

for VIP visits, located on the other side of the woods just behind Elaine's home. The small two-room units had been built away from the complex. "We don't want the owners really seeing how this group lives," Cap had once told Elaine. "That's why we secluded those priority units." He'd chuckled, she remembered. Now she was pleased there had been so much forethought when Glenwood was planned.

"It's perfect," Roland told her a few nights later as they ate dinner at Elaine's. "I just needed a place for my gear. I don't intend to be there much," he added with a wink.

He wanted to know about Glenwood, the team's history, and everything else. He never stopped asking questions after that; it appeared that he wanted to absorb every ounce of information about her and the Hawks.

Most evenings that first week were just spent talking about the past—his, hers, and the team's. She explained how Glenwood was an investment Cap had suggested to the owners years before. Half the complex was made up of rental apartments; the other half was singly owned condos. The income from both subsidized the team.

"And we write off the player housing as expenses. Works great," she told Pantier.

"But you own yours, right?" he questioned.

It was then she told him about Tony and her widowed life. The story came out in summary form, as if her life for those many years had belonged to someone else. Never before had she talked to anyone but Meggan about it. With Roland, however, it was easy to explain, easier than she could have imagined.

He listened and asked questions. That he wanted to know all about Elaine pleased her, and she opened up completely. She told him little anecdotes about Tony's career, how they had come to uncover the antique treasures that filled the house, and how hard it had been to accept his

113

death. Without tears or remorse now, she spoke to Pantier about the dream she had once lived with Tony.

"I've wondered about your past," Pantier said as her story ended. "I couldn't imagine such a lovely Work of Art never having married." He chuckled faintly. "I even quizzed Phil, trying to find out if you had a boyfriend, a fiancé maybe."

"And what did Phil have to say?" She hoped he would tell her exactly what had been said, and he did.

"He made it very clear from the beginning that you were alone. And I still couldn't believe it!"

So that was why he had teased her at Torontino's; he was testing Phil's version of her life.

"I honestly think Phil was trying to advertise your virtues." Roland smirked. "That guy must think I'm blind as well as ancient." They both laughed. "But didn't you find it hard to be married to a prime athlete?" he asked a moment later with intense interest.

"No. Should I have?" She was curious to hear his thoughts.

"I can't imagine a serious contender for big-time hockey having enough stamina to maintain a career *and* a good marriage." He was questioning himself as much as he was her.

"We never thought about it," she replied. "It seemed so natural, like two people being doctors or lawyers. Hockey was a common bond between us, and I think our marriage was stronger because of that bond."

"It must have been one in a million," he said thoughtfully. "I've never believed that pro anythings should get married." He stared into space before continuing slowly. "Athletes are married to their work really." He stopped short of a full explanation, and it was Elaine's turn to probe.

"You've never been married?"

"Not even engaged." It sounded impossible to her.

"But you've had relationships, haven't you?" At that mo-

114

ment Roland was an enigma to her: virile superstar without a romantic past. It was impossible to visualize.

"Yes," he began slowly. "A few. I'm far from being celibate, if that's what you're thinking!" She smiled, and he continued. "I try to be honest. Honest with myself and other people. My work doesn't lend itself to a normal lifestyle. On the road, off the road, injuries, training. What kind of husband or parent, for heaven's sake, could I be with that kind of life?"

His philosophy fascinated her. It was considerate but painful, too. Roland had thought it through completely, she soon discovered, and had decided to concentrate his life on the one thing he was sure of: hockey.

"I'm always honest," he said later. "I try never to hurt anyone. If I think a relationship is going too fast or in the wrong direction, I say so. And that's the only way I can be. Other people have the option of having different lives, an option that I don't feel I can offer honestly."

"You're a real disappointment," Elaine said with a laugh. "I had you pegged for a jet-set playboy from day one!"

"My fans would be shocked," he answered. "Don't let it get around, okay?"

She nodded. They talked of other things. But late that night, as he lay sleeping, she couldn't get their conversation out of her mind. Something about what he'd said disturbed her. Just what it was that kept her awake, she couldn't describe.

Perhaps it was the loneliness inherent in his plan that made her uneasy. It was inconceivable to her. But, then, she'd known other possibilities; she'd had other options.

When morning came, she had conveniently forgotten the conversation.

Elaine had never been a dreamer. Her life before Roland had never afforded such self-indulgent departures from the cold realities of life. Perhaps that was why she indulged herself now, within the fervor of their secret affair. It was wildly different from anything she'd ever known: so carefree, almost insane in its complexity, but abundant in rewards.

For endless weeks she and Roland secretly gloated over the success they'd made of their love affair. Each evening one or the other would slip through the early-winter dusk down the narrow wooded path that separated their condos.

Most of their time together, however, was spent at Elaine's. Not only did they have more room in which to roam, but Elaine's home had all the amenities of television, easy chairs, and most important, a well-equipped kitchen. It didn't take Elaine long to learn that Roland loved to cook.

Within a few weeks Roland had all but abandoned the efficiency apartment in favor of Elaine's more inviting home.

"This is much better," he confided after hanging a few select garments in her spare closet. "With your antiques, the flowers, and all, I feel very much at home. Just like being in Edmonton almost. But there is one problem."

She looked at him blankly.

"Ah, but can't you see?" he said with a sweep of his hand. "I feel like a kept man here."

"What?"

"Oh, yes. Kept. It's an ugly situation," he added with a coy wink. "I can't live under such humiliating circumstances."

"What do you propose?" Elaine asked, beginning to understand his real intention.

"Why, that I contribute to the common coffer, of course. I can't have you bearing all the expense, madame. After all, it's enough that you bear my passion!" They both laughed at the absurdity.

Elaine tried to object, but Roland would hear none of it,

and they ended by agreeing that he would buy the food for the household.

"I think that's fair enough," she said. "After all, you're the one who eats!"

The great Panther retaliated by chasing her through the house, tackling her on the sofa, and tickling her, unmercifully, into surrender.

## CHAPTER SEVEN

Three days before Thanksgiving Elaine sat talking with Coach Holloway in his office as a call came through from the Edmonton home office. She tried to excuse herself, but Cap motioned for her to stay.

"Good morning, George," Cap said into the receiver to the Oilers' coach. "What's your pleasure?" As he pivoted in his chair, Cap's face quickly changed. "Of course," he said and smiled. "When do you want him? Fine, fine. All right. I'll take care of it."

At first Elaine thought Edmonton had decided to call up one of the Hawks' rookies. But the look on Cap's face, as he hung up the phone, told her it was something much more serious.

"They want Pantier back at Edmonton by New Year's," he said to Elaine.

Her heart skipped. His words tore at her, and she felt a sickening weakness in her stomach.

"I'm glad for him, of course," Cap added. "But he was just beginning to whip those rookies into a real team." He sighed and looked at Elaine. "If we could have held on to him for most of the season . . ." His voice trailed off. Elaine knew what he was thinking. Pantier was a remarkable player coach. He was good for the team. But that didn't matter to her. Not now.

Her throat was dry. She bit at her lip. Before Cap could notice her reaction, Elaine rose to leave the office.

118

"Well, we've got to be realistic," the coach said musingly as she opened the door. "Roland deserves being recalled."

"I know." Elaine forced herself to answer. "But how long will it last?" It was only a matter of time before they'd no longer need him.

"For the rest of this season," Cap said, "maybe all of next season. No telling how long really." Elaine nodded and left without further comment.

Back in her own office, Elaine couldn't manage the pain any longer. Her body collapsed against the examining table, and she sobbed into her folded arms. She couldn't think. Only the feeling of intense loss engulfed the moment; she was stranded in despair.

An hour passed. Elaine composed herself enough to carry on a therapy session with Vosienne. Two other consultations drifted by, her conscious mind performing ordinary duties and barely concealing the emotional pain she was enduring.

The long afternoon dragged on. She was passive and undemanding during power skating. And when she completed the absolute minimum her position required, Elaine slipped away from the arena and headed home.

The day had been consumed by a strange emptiness. She felt drained, stunned, and unable to sort out her emotions. Only one thing was clear: In a few short weeks Roland Pantier would be gone—out of her life. By the time she arrived home, her head was throbbing. She took an aspirin and prepared for Roland's arrival. Shortly after dusk he came in.

"How's it goin', sweetie?" he boomed in a voice full of excitement. By his mood she felt certain that Cap had told him about his recall.

"Nothin' new." She tried to sound equally cheerful as she prepared dinner.

"You'll never guess what Holloway told me today." Elaine didn't venture a guess. "I'm going back to

119

Edmonton!" He laughed and grabbed her. "Cap says I'm to play with the Hawks till Christmas just to get back in the swing, and then it's back to major-league play by New Year's."

She kissed his cheek and mustered a genuine smile. Pantier's eyes were twinkling, his skin glowed with excitement, and he looked so happy and relieved that she found herself reinforcing his pleasure. "Did you really think you'd be down on the farm forever?"

"Never!" He kissed her hard. "Do you remember what you told that reporter months back? You prophesied I'd be back for the second half of the season." Pantier gave her a tremendous bear hug. "You were right on target! I guess this scouting job's over for certain."

As he kissed her again and held her against him with ferocious, exuberant strength, Elaine felt a sob forming in her throat. She wanted to cry, to release an unnamed anxiety deep in her soul. Tears formed in her eyes, and she struggled to control them. But they were insistent and suddenly overpowered her. With tears streaming down her cheeks, Elaine held on to Roland and sobbed.

"What's this?" he asked as he pulled her away and searched her face. "This is a celebration, not a funeral, you know."

"I know." She choked out the words. "I'm so happy for you, Roland." And that was true; she was very pleased for him. But how could she explain that his reprieve was painful to her?

"Remind me never to make you this happy again." He laughed. "I don't think either one of us could stand it!"

While she tried to laugh with him and at herself, Elaine was gripped by grief. She knew the feeling well; she'd experienced it only once before, but she recognized it clearly. Another mourning period was beginning.

In the time that they had been together, the passion between them had not diminished. Each touch, each kiss still made her weak with desire. Now, in celebration, he wanted to make love to her once more.

Her silent grief infused their lovemaking with a new energy. As if she could hold back inevitable loss by sheer passion and willpower, Elaine fought to hold him within her, to extract his essence and disarm the very fate that threatened to take him away. But even as they lay together on the sofa, spent and weary, she knew it was useless to try to hold him.

"What's this?" Roland asked, handing her an unopened envelope from the coffee table.

The return address indicated a post office box in Indianapolis. "Probably junk mail," she answered without thinking. Roland tore open the envelope.

It was another letter from the director of the National Sports Medicine Center. Dr. Caswell had known Elaine for a long time, and at first Roland thought his letter was a fund-raising plea. Much to Roland's amazement, it was a very strong personal offer of a position with Caswell's organization.

"This is wonderful!" he exclaimed after reading it over. "Now will you go to talk to this Caswell? This latest offer is extraordinary."

"I don't think so, Roland. I'd like to see the center someday, but I don't think I'm interested in working there."

"Give me one good reason why not," he demanded. "And if you say you can't leave the Hawks, I'll crown you."

"Then crown me," she replied, more uncertain of the offer than annoyed with his insistence. "I like it here. As a senior trainer I can really work with the players. You get involved with these centers and suddenly you're looking a test tube in the face eight hours a day."

"Do you understand the position they're offering you?" he asked. "I doubt that a director of physical therapy spends her day talking to test tubes. That's a people-to-people type of job, Elaine."

"I'll think about it," she said, but her mind wasn't on the subject of sports medicine. Only Roland's leaving for Edmonton occupied her mind at that moment.

"You can't just think about it." He was pressing her hard now. "I don't want to see a talent like yours being wasted on a minor-league team. You have too much to offer. You like to work with younger athletes, right?" She nodded. "Then think of the opportunity being offered you. That center was created to work with kids just getting into sports. Now that's right up your alley. You could really *do* something there. So much of the work is educational that I'll bet you'd be on the road doing education promos most of the time, touching the most important resource we have —young people."

"What would you know about kids?" she snapped. At that moment his comments on marriage surfaced from her memory, making her feel defensive. She was also angry at him, but for what, she didn't know.

He was excited about her job offer and didn't hear the anger in her voice.

"I work a lot with young people," he explained. "I have an old mate who owns a summer hockey camp near Toronto. Each summer I work all three sessions, coaching ten- to fifteen-year-olds. It's great. You'd be good at something like that, too."

"I'd like that," she confessed. "But really, Roland, I'm happy with the Hawks. Cap, Phil, and I are a hard team to beat."

Roland put the letter on the table and leaned back next to her on the sofa. "I've seen that team in action, remember?" His voice was quiet, and he wrapped his arm around her shoulder. "But you can't expect it to go on forever. Cap's nearing retirement, Phil's been offered an assistant coach's job at Edmonton—"

"He has?" She hadn't heard about that. But, then, she'd

been in another world since she'd met Roland and the season had begun.

"That's right; he told me last week." He kissed her cheek. "You can't live in the past forever," he whispered.

"What do you mean?" she asked him, confused again.

"I'm saying that you have to think about your future. You're too limited here. You may like it, always being with the same people and surroundings, but you can't recapture what's past." She knew without having to be told that he was talking about her husband.

"You're wrong, Roland." Her voice was hesitant. Elaine wasn't sure that he *was* wrong, but she didn't feel up to talking about it. Not that evening. Not now.

"Am I wrong?" he went on. "Have you been living a normal life here?"

"And you're an expert on normal living, I suppose," she replied with rising anger.

"I know what's normal for me."

"Then let me determine what's normal for me."

"Do you really know?" he asked her. "Have you thought about it? You're just getting back into life after two years of shutting it out. Open up to other possibilities, Elaine."

"I have," she replied sternly. *And just look what's happened to me*, she thought.

"Then keep going. Don't let old loyalties stand in your way," he told her.

She mused that old loyalties included him as well.

"The world's changing around you. Cap, Phil, even Meggan. Soon there won't be much remaining of the Hawks as you knew them. I just want you to think about a good change for Elaine."

She saw that he was sincere, but it was all too much to think about just then. In the space of one short day her world had been torn apart again. Nothing she could do that night would salvage it.

"I am thinking about Elaine," she said sharply. "But I

prefer to do it in my own way and in my own time." Her head was pounding again, and she was emotionally exhausted. "So let's not discuss it anymore tonight, all right?"

He could only say, "All right, that's fair. But promise me that you'll look into this offer. Please?" "Please" wasn't a word he used often, and she mellowed again.

"I promise."

Their next two weeks together held a special brand of excitement and anxiety. Roland was officially released to play with the Hawks until Christmas. The owners wanted him back in competition, and he was ready to go.

Elaine honestly tried to forget the ominous cloud of gloom that Roland's recall had brought to her. She tried, but fear and grief haunted her.

Each morning he ran with her over their three-mile course. She laughed at his pace, he groaned in appreciation of her concern, and they ate monstrous noon breakfasts.

Roland discovered an aerobics program on cable and supplemented his rigorous workout at the gym with an additional half hour of exercise in front of the television. He tried to encourage Elaine to join in, too, but she was not interested in Terry Thomas's bountiful bosom and took the time to do household chores instead.

When she finished the dishes one bright winter morning, Elaine wandered back through the living room to find Roland standing on tiptoes before the TV. His arms were twitching and bending as he imitated Terry and her merry band of contortionists on the set.

"What is that?" She giggled.

"It's called a butterfly. Great for upper-body blood flow. How do I look?" He panted, wanting her to critique his imitation.

"Like an overloaded DC-nine having takeoff problems!"

"Thanks," he grumbled. "You're so supportive." Elaine grew so weak from laughter that she had to sit down on the floor to watch the rest of his routine. All she could think of was how much she was going to miss him. Every detail of every moment they had left she cherished and commended to memory.

With his renewed vitality and optimism, Roland worked the team into a lather during practice that week. He finally had his opportunity to work the players over, and he didn't take it lightly. As Elaine kept track of the workouts, hidden from view in the highest row above the rink, she grew increasingly pleased with what she saw. Roland had been right. The Hawks needed him on the ice, not on the bench.

By game time the next Saturday she had considered placing a side bet with the Salt Lake City trainer; she was that sure the Hawks would win one fair and square.

She and Roland were still working at keeping their relationship under wraps, but it was getting very hard for Elaine not to show her pride and love for him. He was the most graceful hockey player she'd ever seen, stealing across the ice with powerfully accurate speed and timing. She could understand why he'd been nicknamed the Panther: Roland pounced and ran, cornered and stalked opponents just like a great cat. He was exquisite.

Saturday evening they ventured to drive together to the game. But as soon as they arrived, he headed for the dressing room, and she sprinted to her office to change. As she was packing her med kit, the door opened and Roland crept in.

"Black is your style," she said and kissed him. The uniform and padding still aroused her. She ran her fingers through his hair and rubbed her leg up and down his, just to remind him that he was sexy.

"Don't start up with me." He chuckled. "I have to concentrate on the game."

"Why?" she whispered in his ear. "You'll take care of Salt Lake okay."

"I know, I know, but I want to look interested in the action." Elaine giggled. "I mean the action on the ice!" Roland chuckled, kissed her forehead, and then handed her a package. "Just a little something to celebrate your return to the real world." She took the box, wrapped in candy-striped red and white tissues, and shook it.

"What is it?" she asked, continuing to shake the box.

"You'll find out. I have to get back to the dressing room." He kissed her again and wobbled toward the door on his skates. "Don't forget about after the game. Wait for me outside the dressing room, okay?"

As he closed the door behind him, she heard the final siren sound, signifying that the pregame warm-up session was over. She had fewer than ten minutes to join the players as they returned to the arena for the start of the game.

Quickly checking the contents of her med kit, she threw a towel across her shoulders and took the remaining seconds to open Roland's gift.

She tore off the paper to find a shiny gold gift box, taped shut on the edges. She ripped off the tape and pulled off the lid to find a black cashmere sweater, complete with the Hawks' emblem, conspicuously monogrammed in bright yellow on the front. Laughing with delight, she opened the accompanying card to read a message scribbled in Roland's broad script: "Official Panther Uniform."

"Hurry up, Doc!" Phil Walters's voice pierced the closed door.

"Coming," she shouted, while stuffing the sweater back into its box. She grabbed her med kit and ran out to join the others.

There was no pretense to that evening's game, no possible way for Elaine or Cap to remain cool and aloof from the action. Pantier started the game at the face-off, and it was dynamic, hard-hitting hockey from that point on.

From the minute his skates touched the ice, thousands of fans were on their feet and screaming. Elaine shouted and cheered as well, her voice lost in a sea of voices. Her pain and pride mingled to produce an eerie, mournful sound that only she heard.

Roland was making up for all the times he had had to play spectator, and Salt Lake wasn't prepared for the effect Pantier had on the other Hawks as well.

The game raced on, and though the players were more physical than she liked, Elaine was caught up in the excitement. Even Cap shouted and stamped. The crowd cheered as Hawks took turns plowing over the Eagles and driving hard for the goalie. It was a flurry of frantic color and speed. The crowd stayed on their feet until the end of the period. The Hawks were after a win; Vosienne clouted in their first goal as the buzzer sounded.

Without any injuries to attend to, Elaine bypassed the dressing room and took refuge in her office. Fifteen minutes of solitude was all she needed to recoup from Roland's performance.

Shuffling through the morning mail, she hummed to herself and halfheartedly reorganized her cluttered desk. Meg Holloway cruised in while she was absorbed in nothingness.

"So what did you think of the first period?" asked Meg.

"I thought Stolypovcyk looked terrific!" Elaine answered, knowing that was the gist of Meg's coded question. Not looking up from the note she was reading, Elaine didn't see Meg pick up the gift box and open it.

"Ah, something from Roland?"

Elaine turned quickly to find Meg examining the sweater. Her eyes were round, and she formed a low whistle to punctuate her approval. "You two are quite a pair!"

Elaine felt her face grow warm, but she knew that the blush was more from pride than embarrassment. "He's always teasing," she replied, grabbing the garment from Meg's hands and quickly putting it back in the box. This time she shoved it into her gym bag.

"That's not what I hear. It sounds as if you two have gone past the teasing stage."

Meg's tone, flat and accusing, brought a terse reply from Elaine. "And *just* what have you heard?" She started to add a sharp referral to Meg and Joe's affair, but her friend's retort was too quick and too deadly serious.

"Just what everyone knows about you and Roland," she said, her eyes holding Elaine's gaze with heartfelt concern. "All the players are talking, Elaine. I'm surprised that Dad hasn't gotten wind of it yet."

Elaine swallowed hard and felt a strange, panicky feeling float through her stomach. The reality of Meg's words hit her hard. Like a sleepwalker suddenly awakened from a dream, Elaine stood, speechless, before the younger woman. Frivolous pride vanished; Elaine's face flamed with embarrassment and distress.

"You're like a sister to me, Elaine, and I wouldn't say anything to hurt you. Honestly." Meg's eyes were misty. "But you've got to be more . . ."

"Discreet," Elaine filled in the gap for her. "But I thought we had been," she said, bewildered and shaken.

Meggan reached out and held her arm. "I know that's what you thought. *I* didn't even know how involved you were," she said. "I never saw him enter or leave your place once. I swear."

"Then how . . ." Elaine couldn't finish the sentence.

"I don't know really. But Joe told me that Vosienne has been making a habit of keeping track of Roland, ever since he moved out on Claude, I guess."

"And now the whole team knows. Right?"

"I'm afraid so. Vosienne's trying to make points with the other guys. You know how it is. He's in the know, and the younger guys are eating up the gossip. Makes him big man on campus with the other rookies."

"Just the rookies?" Elaine had to ask, even though she knew the answer.

"Well, no. But the other guys have worked with you a season or two—some more. Anyway, they don't seem so hot on listening to his tall tales. They like and respect you, Elaine. Everyone does. It's just, well, I thought you should know, that's all. Dad might not take it so gracefully. You know how he is about the coaching staff's setting an example for the team."

How well she knew.

"Listen, Elaine." Meg broke the silence by squeezing Elaine's arm and speaking in a warm, apologetic voice. "I know I haven't any right to be saying all this to you. I've been spending every night with Joe, and we've been so happy—just like you and Roland, I'm sure. But it's different somehow." She looked beyond Elaine's eyes and let go of her arm. "I don't have a career—not like yours, where it matters—and everyone's used to my being dingy—"

"You're not *dingy*," Elaine interrupted her with a hug. "You're just young and full of it. And I love you, Meg." She felt like crying but didn't want to make Meggan feel any worse than she did. "And you're a dear friend. I know how much it took for you to come in here and tell me all this."

The buzzer sounded for the second period, and Elaine picked up her med kit.

"What are you going to do?" Meg asked as they walked back through the crowded hall.

"I don't know. Honestly I don't." They parted with Meg giving her an encouraging smile. Elaine tried to return it with confidence, but she found it hard to manage.

The second period of play continued, but the color and excitement of the game eluded her. Only once was she plunged back into reality when a player went down after a cross-checking, and she was rushed onto the ice to assist. His face was badly bruised, but nothing was broken. She okayed him for play and returned to the bench and her thoughts.

Nothing seemed to make sense for the longest time.

Flashes of remorse, memories, and anxiety just bumped into one another, then flew in a thousand directions. Her mind blurred in a jumble of feelings. She glanced to see Pantier engrossed in the action. He was oblivious to her confusion—safe and sheltered in his own world.

What to do? How? Why? That was it. She had finally stumbled onto a word that categorized the panic inside. Why? Why had she been so stupid? Why had she ever let it go this far? Then other companion questions flooded in: how, when, and *where?* Where had her mind been? Surely she'd lost her mind. That had to be it. She was insane. Simple as that; she was crazy.

When the second period ended, she again bypassed her dressing-room rounds. This time she was trying to hide from everyone and everything except the thoughts that began to accuse and judge her in rapid-fire succession.

She locked the door to her office this time; she wanted no intrusion. Leaning against the examining table, chin in hand, Elaine felt the tears welling up in her closed eyes. Frustration, guilt, and uncertainty added to the well-formed image in her mind of a mature woman reduced to a life pattern of give-and-go love plays.

Deeply angry, she began to punish herself mentally with unnecessary brutality. She produced a detailed vision of herself encouraging Roland's desire and then flaunting the conquest. Years of hard work and integrity gone. Gone. Her brain rang with the thought. All those young men she'd counseled and worked with, encouraged to perfection by example. The trust and confidence Cap had in her. What did they think of her now?

Finally, she gained control of herself. "That's enough," she whispered in the darkness. "Calm down. Get real."

She found a box of tissues and gently dabbed at the tears in her eyes. No one was going to know she'd been wallowing in self-pity. No one. She had every right to be angry at herself, but there had to be a limit to that anger. Gently she coaxed herself back to reality. She had accidentally wounded her pride and was overreacting. Between the two of them, she and Roland would find a solution. She would wait and talk to him about it.

"Okay," she said to herself while rinsing her face with cold water, "you've made a mistake. Now think. What can you do to correct it?"

Composed again, she began to think more rationally. And as she returned to the bench for the third period, Elaine searched for constructive solutions.

Still, as the game concluded, she had been unable to get much beyond the self-abasement. Meg's observations had dealt her pride a severe blow, and Elaine felt foolish and shamed by her own behavior.

"Going to Murphy's?" Meggan asked as she entered Elaine's office after the game.

"I don't know," replied Elaine. "I don't feel much like celebrating." She packed her gym bag.

"Come on," Meg said, noticing Elaine's silent rejection. "Everyone's just going to relax and mingle. It'll be a great way to get your mind off things for a while."

"I know. Roland expects me to go. But I don't know if it's such a good idea now. I mean—"

"I know what you mean, and no one's going to think a thing about you two being together tonight. Not at Murphy's. Don't get paranoid, Elaine. Everybody's going —even Phil's wife. You know how it will be. The guys will be signing autographs and replaying the game. Nobody will even notice us."

"Aren't you going with Joe?"

"Yes and no. He'll drive me there, and he'll drive me home, but that's just about all. Come on." She gently urged Elaine once more. "You and I can sit in a corner and try to figure out some plays of our own. Maybe we can come up with some ideas about you and Roland. All's not lost."

Meggan's childlike face beamed. Everything was simple

and predictable for her. And Elaine needed her optimism more than ever that night.

"All right, you talked me into it," she said and zipped up her bag. "Roland wants me to meet him by the dressing room. Look for me at Murphy's, and save me a seat."

While she waited among the few remaining fans outside the dressing room, Elaine noticed that some of Meg's hopefulness had, indeed, rubbed off. At least she could casually smile and speak to the players as they appeared and not feel self-conscious or ridiculous.

She watched autographs being signed and enjoyed the children's faces as a player posed for a photo or two with them, then strolled away. By the time Roland came out, the crowd had begun to dissipate, but he was still caught up in handshakes and signatures for nearly ten minutes. Finally, he pulled away, bringing one of the Salt Lake City players with him, and the three of them walked out to the parking lot.

"Elaine, this is Jacques Brouillion. Jacques, this is Elaine D'Arte, the Hawks' trainer. Jacques used to be with Edmonton." He made his introductions when they were seated in the car and speeding along toward Murphy's. He didn't need to explain further about Brouillion. He'd obviously been traded down and out of the majors.

"Madame, *mon plaisir,*" the burly goalie said from the back. "Roland says you are beautiful." He moved up and peered longingly at her from between the bucket seats. "But he lies! You are magnificent! Why do you lie, Roland? Eh?"

His unabashed compliment was not a pleasant one, and she expected Roland to put the player in line. Instead, he encouraged him.

"Why should I tell you all my secrets, Brouillion?" Roland replied and patted Elaine's leg. "This I keep for myself!" He squeezed her thigh and ran his large hand down to her knee, while laughing at the ignoble face Brouillion was making in the rearview mirror.

"Perhaps I can make a trade this season. I think I like Omaha. Much better staff than the Great Salt Lake, no?"

She found the goalie's comment rude, but Roland's thundering laughter was almost obscene, and she was overcome with a blistering anger again. Throwing his hand off her leg, she tried to ignore both of them.

"Ah, she is spunky, Roland!" exclaimed Brouillion, seeing her force Roland's hand back. "An Italian tiger for the Panther. Marvelous! Marvelous!"

By the time they reached Murphy's, Elaine was smoldering. Her anger was now focused on Roland, who seemed to enjoy the goalie's jokes at her expense thoroughly.

Angry as she was, Elaine had not lost her perspective; she had to talk to Roland and tell him what Meggan had said.

Just as they entered Murphy's, she pulled him away from Brouillion and into a recess near the phone booth.

"I have to talk to you," she said quickly. "Alone!" she exclaimed.

Roland shrugged and motioned to Brouillion to go on in. "Join you in a minute," he added, and Brouillion went on into the pub.

"What is it?" Roland asked, appearing more uninterested than annoyed. "Can't you wait till we get home?"

"No," Elaine whispered. "It can't wait. Everyone knows about—" She stopped to take a deep breath before continuing. Calmer, she began again. "Meg says that the whole team knows about us, Roland. She made a point of telling me during the period break at the game."

Roland's eyes never focused on her; he was distracted, only half listening to her.

"All right. Okay," he mumbled, searching the pub room beyond for Brouillion.

"Hey, Pantier!" someone shouted. "What's keepin' you?"

"Be there in a second," he called back with a smile. "We'll talk later," he said to Elaine, who was now too angry to speak. "It can wait; let's join the party." He hooked his arm in hers and pulled Elaine into the pub room. Fortunately—for him—he was detained by several fans as they walked in, and she was unable to retaliate.

Meg waved at her from a back booth, and Elaine elbowed her way through the crowd.

"What's the matter?" asked Meg. "Your face is scarlet!"

"It's that Eagles' goalie," Elaine replied, trying to cover up her anger at Roland's callous reaction.

"Oh, you mean Bruiser Brouillion. Did you meet him?"

"I met him, and he *will* be bruised if he gets within ten feet of me again." Then she explained the car scene without skipping a detail.

"Careful, Elaine," Meg cautioned. "You really aren't in a very good space tonight. You know how the players get. They're all hyped up from the game. Roland's just proud of you, that's all. And he's getting a kick out of the other guys' looking you over."

"I'm not a piece of meat, Meggan," Elaine said sharply, not at all soothed by Meg's objectivity.

Elaine had begun to get a better perspective on things. Sitting and watching the normal spectacle of hockey players trying to impress one another and burly fans, captivated by hoopla, milling about the bar, she found herself forming quite a different picture of herself and Roland.

How stupid she had been, thinking she was to blame for encouraging *him*. Clearly, her mind calculated, she had fallen into *his* little scheme.

All along she thought that his enticements were a test of her courage. What absolute, irrational bunk. He'd wanted her from the moment they'd met. Another conquest for the supercat.

134

Her thoughts made her sick at heart as she realized how she'd set herself up for all of this.

"Fear dragon . . . phooey," she mumbled.

"What did you say?" Meg asked, thinking she was talking to her.

"Nothing. I didn't say anything to you." *No*, she thought, *I'm having a very private talk with myself.*

By the time it dawned on her just how ridiculous the whole process had been, Elaine was furious: furious at Roland and even angrier at herself. Wasn't it obvious, by the way he'd exhibited her to Brouillion, that she was just another athletic trophy? No wonder he didn't care that the whole team knew about them! Roland was probably enjoying the notoriety of it all—and at her expense. How dare he just brush her aside and say the problem could wait?

"I'm leaving," she said suddenly to Meg. "Did you drive?"

"No, but I can get Joe's keys." By the look on Elaine's face, Meggan knew better than to question her. She had seldom seen Elaine angry, but she recognized the volcanic activity rising in her friend's eyes. "I'll get the keys."

Meg pushed her way to where Stolypovcyk stood munching popcorn and giggling at another player's animated joke; forcefully Elaine made her way toward the door. Halfway across the floor, she was intercepted by Brouillion. He put one arm around her shoulder and literally lifted her into a small circle of players.

"This, my good fellows, is Monsieur the Panther's latest *squeeze*, Madame D'Arte." Everyone laughed. Brouillion held her tightly in place and grinned down at her.

Through the circle of bodies she caught sight of Pantier. Surrounded by admiring fans, he was too busy playing superjock to be aware of Elaine's predicament, much too engrossed in his stardom to be even concerned about her.

Her anger soared at the thought, and without a second's hesitation Elaine planted her left foot squarely across the toes of Brouillion's right foot, with every ounce of strength she had. "Squeeze *that!*" she said as he bellowed in pain and grabbed his foot. The group now stood laughing at Brouillion, and Elaine marched triumphantly out the door, neither looking for Pantier again nor even caring if he knew she had left.

Elaine appreciated Meg's silence on the short drive home. Meggan didn't try to cajole Elaine into light conversation, and she didn't try to reason with her either. Small talk and reason were the farthest two topics from Elaine's mind.

As they pulled up in front of her condo, Elaine managed a neutral "thanks" and went in without further comment.

She'd had enough of Pantier and his devil-may-care attitude. And in one single evening she'd had enough of his mindless disregard for her feelings and her career. Of course, he wasn't worried about their romance being public knowledge. Why would he be concerned now? After all, he'd been recalled to Edmonton; he'd be away from the problem soon enough. In a matter of weeks Elaine would be left to face the consequences on her own.

Yes, she'd had enough.

After dumping her gym bag in the bedroom, she paced from room to room, armed with a paper grocery sack. Every trace of Roland's presence had to be removed. Though illogical, even petty, her rampant desire to clean him out of her life seemed more appropriate than slamming doors or throwing dishes. And so, with meticulous attention, she hunted for any and all remnants—anything that might remind her later that he had ever been there.

There was *his* copy of *The Hockey News* and *his* coffee cup, which suspiciously matched the others in her set, but it, too, was dumped, without ceremony into the waiting sack. In the living room he'd left a pair of gloves, which she tossed away, along with the zebra plant—complete with pot and companion soil—that he'd given her the day before. From the refrigerator she even pulled the leftover quiche that he'd made for dinner and plopped it into the bag—sans Tupperware container.

Certain that not a trace of him remained, Elaine carefully folded over the top of the sack several times, carried it out the front door, and dropped it on the ground to await final disposal the next morning. She closed the door, feeling somewhat better, as if a painful memory had been justly prepared for demolition.

The anger was subdued for the time being, and she decided to shower and wash her hair just for good measure.

Emerging from the bath, hair tied in towel and swathed in a terry robe, she tuned in the late, late weekend movie. The dialogue distracted her fairly effectively, and she was making cocoa and listening to the old movie when Roland knocked at the front door.

She *knew* it was he by the knock. Slowly she removed the cocoa from the burner, turned down the television, and opened the door as he began to knock again.

"Where'd you go?" he questioned as he rushed in, kissed her cheek, and began to unbutton his coat. "I looked all over for you. Don't tell me you hurried home just to wash your hair." He kissed her again, not noticing either her silence or the stony glare she'd prepared for him.

"I came home," she answered flatly. "And you're going home yourself right now."

"What's the matter?" he asked, wrapping his arms around her. "Do you get keyed up after games, too?"

She pushed his arms away and backed up. "I do *not* get keyed up over games, I get angry when I'm treated like a common camp follower by bozo hockey players."

He smiled, not realizing the depth of her anger, and tried once more to embrace her. "Did you let Brouillion get to you, my little Work of Art?" She tried to pull away from him again, but he held her this time. "You can't blame a guy for appreciating a thing of beauty when he sees one."

"Brouillion is a goon; I wouldn't expect any less from his type. I've taken care of passes before." Elaine just glared at him but kept her voice low yet seething as he held her by the arms.

"I know. Joe told me what you did to his foot." Pantier chuckled, then turned serious. "But really, Elaine, you should be more careful; you could have broken his toes."

"I'll break more than his toes if he ever lays a hand on me again!"

"Ah, now I get to see that Italian temper of yours at work, eh?" He tried to kiss her, but she slipped under his arms instead and backed away once more. "Come on, Elaine, you're a big girl. Surely this run-in with Brouillion couldn't have made you so unreasonable."

"Unreasonable? Brouillion? No, that jerk didn't faze me. But your treating me like just another chippy was another story!" He hadn't really been listening to her. And if he hadn't taken her seriously before, she was about to make certain he didn't miss the point again.

"I won't have you *handling* me like a piece of equipment again, Roland. What was all that in the car? Rubbing my leg and egging Brouillion on. How could you let him talk to me like that? Who—or, better yet, what—do you think I am?" Roland now stood quietly in front of her. His smile had dissolved into a straight, tight line, and his eyes narrowed with understanding. Finally, he realized just how upset Elaine really was. "Well?" she prodded.

"I'm sorry, Elaine. You're right. I did overdo it. But I didn't mean to embarrass you. Honestly. I was just up, you know." He tried to touch her, but she turned away and closed the door.

"Is that why you deserted me at Murphy's, too? Just up?" Her anger took hold, and she listened to her words as they grew harsher and more cutting. She projected all the hurt and confusion she felt on Roland.

138

"I didn't desert you. It's always like that. You could have joined in, you know, instead of leaving in a huff!"

"You haven't seen my huff yet," she told him. "I'm nobody's *squeeze*, Pantier. Is that how you refer to me? Did you tell Brouillion I was your latest squeeze?"

His brows knitted coarsely, and his eyes flashed, but Roland's voice remained cool as he answered, "We're adults, Elaine. Adults get involved; they have affairs if they're attracted to one another. I never referred to you as anything but Elaine. *Mon Dieu*, you're acting like a teen-age crazy. Everyone knows we've been together. Start acting your age."

His objective, if not subtle, remark was all she needed, and the anger, frustration, and pain erupted headlong.

"That's just it. Everyone does know, and I *am* acting my age. I'm not a teen-age crazy; I'm a woman of thirty-two who enjoys her privacy. And if you could act *your* age, we wouldn't be having this conversation." She crossed her arms and accentuated her point with confirmed silence.

His great dark eyes stared at her; he buttoned his coat and walked to the door. "Is that really it?" he asked, turning back to her. "Is it just your privacy you're worried about, or have you suddenly gotten cold feet? I didn't exactly force you to make love with me. We both wanted it if I'm not mistaken. Or is this a common affliction? Do you just tire that easily of a man? Or is it a hit-and-miss game all widows play?"

With a resounding crack her palm struck his cheek. Roland didn't wince. He just walked out and closed the door behind him.

## CHAPTER EIGHT

Righteous anger sustained her that night, and Elaine fell into a troubled sleep, her hand still smarting from the slap she'd delivered to Roland. But when she woke early the next morning, the anger had worn away, to reveal much more than she wanted to accept.

She puttered around the house, read the Sunday paper, and drank coffee for hours, trying to avoid any thought of Roland and the night before, but she was strangely agitated all the same. Her mind was restless, and she was not at ease with the slow morning ritual.

After having eaten a light brunch and read everything of interest to her in the paper, she decided to jog. Maybe if she ran fast enough and hard enough, the natural rhythm of her mind and body would return. She threw on a sweat suit and started out in hard, long strides.

It was unusually cold, even for late November; a light, freezing mist was falling, and the sky was gray and cloudy. Still, she really didn't notice. She concentrated solely on her legs as they pumped out the tired blood and stretched her muscles.

She didn't bother to pace herself. The harder she ran, the less she thought about anything else. But by the time she'd run into the woods, her legs were aching, and she slowed down to a stationary jog and rested.

Snow began to fall. *It's early this year*, she thought, watching the crystalline flakes falling lightly over the dead leaves. Her step was spongy on the damp ground, so she decided to walk back.

Wind and snow stung at her eyes, and tears formed. Yet it wasn't the cold but an intense feeling of loss that made her cry. Where anger had given her the courage to break off their relationship, tears now tried to wash away a deep feeling of remorse that invaded her mind. Bright crystal tears mixed with the snow against her cheeks in the icy air.

The condo was warm and bright; she was glad to get back before anyone saw her. How could she possibly explain what she was feeling when she didn't really understand it herself? No one would understand; it was a blessing that no one had seen her walking along in the cold, crying.

After taking off the damp sweat suit, she put on her robe, whisked away a remaining tear, and began to search for something to take her mind off Pantier and the emptiness. She found a small oak shelf, salvaged from a flea market, in the spare bedroom and carried it into the living room. She spread newspapers on the floor in front of the television and settled down to watch a football game and sand years of varnish and grime from the little antique whatnot.

Listlessly she scoured the wood and tried to get involved with the action of the game, but the afternoon dragged on without getting any better. Somehow she felt like the used wood in her hands. With each stroke of the sandpaper, Elaine tried to abrade the memories, the dulled varnish of her own life. After a few hours the shelf was bare, clear wood again, and Elaine, too, had begun to release some of the lusterless traces of memory that had led to Roland's banishment.

She almost called him once. She went as far as dialing all but the last two digits of his number before hanging up. She wanted to tell him something; just what, she wasn't sure. No, it was better this way, she thought. Better to have ended it now, even in anger, than to have it . . . What? To have it what?

141

Eventually she began to see what had really set her off. It wasn't the possibility of Cap's finding out, perhaps reprimanding her at most. It wasn't even the fact that the players knew, although she realized she had to be very concerned with image. Not at all. Those were all minor compared to the acknowledgment that she had been one more woman in a long list of Pantier *squeezes*. Even the word made her cringe.

Elaine did not want to compromise, to be just another woman in his life.

She hadn't felt like that about *him*. Their time together had been more than just an interlude—at least to her. It was having to face the reality of it all that had made her so angry.

Elaine looked at the antique rocker by the window. Roland had claimed it, just as Tony had, years before. She could see Pantier sitting there, now, peering out into the world from behind the plants and talking to her about *his* dreams.

They had spent many happy hours just talking and dreaming. Roland philosophized on everything from sports to cooking; his life, as hers, had developed into a strong pattern of beliefs and objectives. She remembered how sure he always sounded and how she'd admired him for it.

It had all occurred in that very room. Roland had rocked by the window, while she worked at some project on the floor. It had seemed so right, perfect. Why couldn't it have stayed that way for just a little while longer? But then Elaine knew that even a temporary reprieve wouldn't have satisfied her. She wanted him in her life forever, as a partner, not just as a seasonal lover.

In the solitude of that snowy afternoon she missed him very much. How just one month could have made such a difference was baffling. For two years her life had been even, structured. Without Tony, Elaine had created a new

142

life—one that was satisfying and productive. How could two years have been displaced overnight? She had been happy and contented with her life just as it was. Everything she needed had been supplied by her job and friends. Or had it? What was it that Pantier had brought into her life that was indispensable, special?

What was it, and why did it have to be so temporary, so meaningless to him? Surely, she gave herself credit, it was more than just physical pleasure that had enticed her to fall deeply in love with him. Or could she have wanted a man's body that badly? That was one thought that she couldn't—wouldn't—entertain. She wasn't what he had said: a desperate widow. She was *not* planning to spend the rest of her life in give-and-go—hit-and-run—affairs.

Her love for him was genuine and far exceeded passion alone. That was but an added luxury. No, Elaine loved his spirit and determination, his joy and boundless energy. And his mind. Oh, yes, how he reasoned everything out and weighed each fact. She loved that, too. It was a reflection of his soul. Life was precious to him, and he tried to extract every ounce of energy it brought to him daily.

And he had shared it all with her. Roland had given her some of his spirit and hope, and she was now having to face life again without that bountiful gift he made so freely.

Without him her life might return to its sameness. He would not be part of her vast tomorrows.

More bitterly she thought that he would find someone else to share himself with, as he had done before meeting her. Another woman might be given his joy and spirit. Possibly he would choose someone who didn't see the value of it all; perhaps Roland's gifts would be unappreciated, even squandered by a person who didn't love him as Elaine did.

The pitiful vision of his being used and unloved brought more tears and even greater despair to her.

It was early evening when Meggan came over, and much

to Elaine's relief, she interrupted the mental purging. Elaine wanted company—another human being to help break the endless maze of mental gymnastics that had held her captive all day.

"Hi!" Meg bounded in and tried to hand Elaine the grocery sack she'd locked out the night before. "Does this belong to you?"

"It's trash," she replied, and Meg dropped the sack outside before she came in.

"I thought Roland might be here and we could play cards or something."

"Where's Joe?" asked Elaine as she gathered up the newspapers and brushed sawdust from the carpet.

"Oh, he's taking in a movie with a couple of the other guys tonight, says he needs a little space." She took off her coat and tossed it across the sofa. "Aren't you and Roland doing something tonight?"

As she finished speaking, Meg saw the miserable look on Elaine's face.

"Did he request some space, too?" she asked while she followed Elaine into the kitchen.

"He didn't have to ask. I offered. Last night."

"Oh, no. Did you two have a fight because of what I told you? Oh, Elaine, I never meant to upset you. Damn." Meggan flopped into a chair, looking glum.

"Have you eaten?" asked Elaine. "I was about to have something. What would you like?"

"Bread and water. I deserve it."

"No, you don't. Come on, eat with me." It was her turn to coax Meggan. "And stop looking as if you've shot someone. It wasn't your fault at all. It was bound to happen sooner or later, and I just chose to make it *sooner*, that's all."

"But why? You both seemed so happy. Or was it just because you were afraid that Dad would find out? Maybe I made too much out of the whole thing. I shouldn't have mentioned it to you. I'm really sorry, Elaine."

"Don't be sorry. And I wasn't all that worried about Cap," she said, taking a container of sauce and a dozen frozen meatballs from the freezer. "How about spaghetti and meatballs? Five thousand unnecessary calories ought to make us both feel a lot better."

Elaine began to work at dinner, accepting Meggan's silence as a meeting of their minds. It was snowing harder now, and she looked out onto the lawn at the deep white coverlet that had fallen during the day. The whole world seemed clean, ready to begin its long hybernation. And at that moment Elaine wished she, too, felt as free and peaceful as the world outside her window.

"I don't suppose you will be any angrier at me if I ask you another question." Meg broke into Elaine's meditation.

"Go ahead, shoot," replied Elaine, stirring the sauce and somehow wanting to talk it out.

"If you weren't that concerned about Dad or your job, what was it? I mean, how could you just end something that made you so happy? Did Roland do something that awful? I just can't understand it, Elaine." At times Meg Holloway was much more perceptive than her twenty-six years could account for. This was one of those times, and Elaine looked into her wide blue eyes and saw genuine concern.

"Listen, Meg, it's not something he *did* or *didn't* do; it wouldn't be fair of me to push all the blame off on Roland. It's just that it all came into focus last night, and I decided to stop kidding myself, that's all." She continued to cook, but her mind began to form words and images. Finally, after a whole day of dizzy thinking, she was able to find the words to explain it all.

"How did you kid yourself? Huh?" asked Meg. "Being happy is hard to fake."

"No, I don't think either one of us was faking that. He's the kind of guy who's just easy to like and have fun with. But that's all."

145

"Did he say that, or did you think that? Was he just out joyriding?"

"Of course."

"Did he *say* that?"

Meg's cross-examination made Elaine uncomfortable, but she didn't intend to sidestep it. In some strange way Meggan was helping Elaine sort out the jumble of thoughts that still cluttered her mind.

"No, he didn't *say* it. It just couldn't have been more than that. He's leaving Omaha in a month, and then it's back to Edmonton again. I don't know what I was thinking, Meg. I honestly feel so silly and adolescent. A grown woman acting like an infatuated teen-ager or worse." Some of the self-generated anger began to spill out, and she let it flow. "You saw his come-on with me. And I fell for it—hook, line, and hockey stick. Damn. I can be so dumb."

"Is that why you're mad? Mad at yourself for having enjoyed a little romance, for taking a chance and adding some excitement to your life? I don't call that dumb, Elaine. That's *being alive* and *liking* it at the same time."

"Oh, Meggan"—Elaine sighed—"if I were your age—"

"Don't throw that boloney at me," she interrupted. "I get so tired of hearing you use that. We're only five years apart. That doesn't exactly put us in different generations. I think you use that maturity malarkey as a defense." Then, with measured accuracy, she added, "I really believe that you're afraid to risk falling in love again."

Elaine stopped stirring and listened without reply as Meg continued in a soft, diplomatic tone. "I saw how Roland came on to you, but more important, I saw how you responded. And it wasn't adolescent. He sparked something; it was in your eyes. And no one in her right mind could have missed the difference it made in you. You haven't been silly or frivolous. You were just relaxed and honestly happy. And I can tell you that it had everyone

146

talking. Dad, Phil, all the old-timers of the team—we all noticed it. And no one was laughing, I swear."

She walked over to where Elaine still stood, before the bubbling skillet, and put her arms around her. "You're very special to all of us, Elaine, and seeing that light back in your eyes made us all happy for you." She hugged her. "Maybe I shouldn't have said anything last night, but I just wanted you to be careful, that's all."

They hugged each other tightly. "Thank you, Meg. I appreciate your caring," Elaine finally said. They both brushed tears from their eyes, and Meg began to set the table.

"Has he called today?" she asked when they sat down to eat.

"No. But I almost called him."

"Why didn't you? Huh? Just talk it out. It can't be all that bad. What did you argue about anyway?"

"It was really ridiculous. Didn't make much sense even at the time."

Elaine had set the table, and dinner was ready. She sat down across from Meggan and began to tell her about what had happened. Somehow Elaine wanted to explain it all, hoping she would discover more insight or courage about her decision through exploring it once more.

"So, you see," Elaine concluded, "it wasn't just something that happened accidentally. We planned the entire thing. For five whole weeks I've been going right along with the plotting, conspiring right along with Roland to keep our little affair quiet. No wonder he thinks I'm just like all the others he's been with. I've acted the part very well." Then she clarified her thought. "But I didn't realize it. Honestly. Being with him was so . . . good." Her mind wouldn't accept a word with more meaning than "good." "That's why I feel so foolish now. I can't believe I've done this all to myself."

"And what do you think he's feeling right now?" Meg

147

finally asked, having been totally silent up to that point in Elaine's story.

"Anger," she said. "I'm certain he's angry at me, and he has every right to be. After our first night together—when it became clear just how complicated it could be—he gave me the option of ending it, for my own sake, right then."

"What did you say?"

"I said no, that I wanted to live my own life. Now he has to be angry at me. And justifiably. After all, when the going got rough, I backed out. Not very noble of me, was it?" Elaine's face was rueful.

"So clear it up and get back together. Or won't your pride let you be the one to call him and talk it over?"

"It wasn't pride," Elaine said. "I've really thought it over, and it's best to leave it this way."

"For heaven's sake, why?" Meg asked.

"Because there's no future in it. That's why. I'm not interested in being a casual lover for anyone. Not even Roland."

"A few weeks are better than nothing at all," Meg replied as if it were a logical, practical inevitability.

"Maybe for other people, but not for me. It never has been." Elaine poured more coffee and sat down again. "Is that how it is with you and Joe? No commitment, no future?" she asked.

"No." Meg's answer was quick and positive. "I love him."

"But how can you be sure? You only just met him. How can you be sure so quickly?"

"I just know, that's all. And he feels the same way. We just clicked. I don't know how to explain it, Elaine, but neither of us has ever felt this way before. We just know."

Elaine saw that Meg was telling her what she believed to be true. It had never been like Meg to get intimately involved with players; her feeling for Joe must be very different—important.

"But doesn't it make you uneasy to think it might not

really be love? I just can't imagine falling in love at first sight." Although she had asked the question, wanting a justification, Elaine immediately sensed the answer. It was within her, waiting.

"How long did you know Tony before you realized you loved him?" Meg asked.

"I can't remember really. A season maybe." *No, no,* Elaine thought, *it must have been longer.*

"And then how did it happen? Did you look at each other at high noon one day and say, 'I think I've fallen in love with you'? Or did you feel it all the while and then suddenly realize it?" Elaine's mind was miles away, trying to remember. "Don't bother trying to recall it," Meg said. "There's no way to remember. That's just it. It happens. We never remember when or how, but all of a sudden we know it. So what difference does it make if two people recognize it at first sight or not? The point is, you know it sooner if you're open to it and not trying to avoid or deny it. Falling in love isn't a rational process."

Either Elaine was confused, or Meggan was beginning to make a great deal of sense. She chose to accept the latter.

"All right, I see your point. And I'm happy for you and Joe. But it's always been different for me. I've always needed time to get to know a man."

"How many men have you known?" Meg giggled, knowing full well that Tony had been the only love in Elaine's life.

Elaine giggled, too. "That was an open net shot!" She laughed. "You caught me off the ice with that one. How about some dessert?"

"Pass. I'm stuffed." But Elaine walked to the refrigerator and found the ice cream. Meg could see that she was still upset; she ate like this only when something was really bothering her. Yet the younger woman decided to let her friend take the lead. Maybe she would tell her the rest of the story without prodding.

"Cookie?"

"No. Do you know you'll have to run fifty miles to burn off all this food?" Meg said chidingly.

"It's ten miles, and I'll think about that tomorrow." Elaine sat back down at the table, but she was smiling now. "Well, then," she said, "is this thing between you and Joe marriage bound?"

"I don't know. We haven't talked about it. But I'm willing to risk it. He's worth it. Besides, I'd rather risk being hurt than never risk at all."

Elaine bit into a cookie and looked at Meg. "And you think that I'm afraid of risking—is that what you're trying to say?"

"Yep." Meggan reached over and took a cookie. "It's better to have loved and lost . . ."

"Geez, Meg, you're getting too heavy, even for me!" But Elaine had heard her, and even though she didn't want to say it, she knew Meg was perfectly correct. "Listen, I have loved, remember? And as for *risking*, that little dragon got me involved with Pantier in the first place!"

"Run that by me again," Meg said, looking puzzled.

Elaine told her how she handled uncertainty in her life. "When I'm not being positive or when I'm confronted with a situation I don't understand, I sit down, analyze it, and try to name the fear it represents. Simple. I call them dragons in my mind."

"Sounds plausible," Meg commented.

"It is. When Roland first came on to me, I couldn't get away fast enough. Then I got to studying it, and I came to believe that I *was* afraid of risking again. I dropped my defenses and wham—here I am, regretting it."

"Why are you regretting it? It sounds as if you've enjoyed the experiment, and now the future should be better, fuller because of it."

"But I've run out of time, Meg. Can't you understand?

The effort, the risking have been wasted on someone who meant to be in my life for only a few short months!"

"Why is time so important to you, Elaine? What can be the harm in enjoying love whenever and wherever it happens? And you know Roland isn't going to Mars or Saturn; he's going a couple of hundred miles north. It doesn't have to end when he returns to Edmonton. Think of all you have in common with each other. There's always the other six months of the year, when neither one of you is tied up working."

Elaine was surprised at how encouraging Meg's rationale was. Her speech almost made her believe there was more to the relationship than she had proof of. Still, she could almost instantly see the loopholes that appeared in Meggan's logic.

"Listen to me for a minute," she interjected as Meg took a well-deserved breath. "Maybe with someone else all this could be true. But not with Pantier. He keeps telling me—and anyone else who'll listen—that all he wants out of life is to play pro hockey. Remember category number two?"

"Sure, sure, they're the never-marrying ones who live to play hockey—"

"And that's Roland. It doesn't mean that he's a terrible human being. It just means that he knows what he wants. Maybe in some ways he's brighter than I am. I've been down all day because I can't have my cake and eat it too."

"That's not true, Elaine." There was sheer determination in Meg's voice. "If you love each other and make each other happy—for a week or a whole season—it doesn't matter. What's important is the loving."

"Now that *is* true," Elaine replied. "But he doesn't love me, and I'm not willing to give myself to anyone—for a week or even a season—who doesn't really love me. I'm just chalking this up to a fling, and I've decided I don't like *flings*."

It came out as easily as that. And Elaine was immediately

embarrassed by the realization. She turned hot pink and tried to detour the conversation by clearing the table of dishes.

"Do you love him?" Meggan asked slowly.

Elaine had expected the question but didn't want to answer it. Plates rattled into the sink, and Elaine returned to the table for more.

"I love him so much that it hurts," she said almost in a whisper.

If she had stopped lying to herself, then Elaine wasn't going to lie to Meggan.

Just when Elaine had relaxed enough to sleep, the alarm clock signaled the start of a new day. Unrested and slightly hung-over from emotional swings throughout the night, she was almost relieved at being able to get up and move once more.

Turning on WOW, she gave Meg's words one last thought, and as she got into the shower, she vowed to put it all on automatic pilot. She was exhausted from having mentally mauled her own feelings. It was time to work at what she had and to forget what she didn't have.

Wind and snow rumbled around the windows; winter was upon her. She felt like jogging, but as she prepared breakfast and listened to the weather report, Elaine decided to skip it that morning. Instead, she hurried through her egg and coffee and decided to get to the arena early and skate off the spaghetti and ice cream before anyone else arrived.

Although her closet still held the same old routine sweat suits, she picked out a bright blue one to wear to work. Something, she thought, to brighten her spirits. The forgotten gym bag still lay on the floor where she had tossed it on Saturday night. Elaine picked it up and dumped the full contents onto the carpet, preparing to repack.

A gold box fell open at her feet, and the black sweater

spilled across the floor. She picked it up, astonished at the rush of sentiment it brought back. With a sigh Elaine slowly refolded it, placed it back within the tissue of its box, and stretched to place the box on a high shelf in the closet where she stored her other mementos. It seemed appropriate to put Roland's gift next to the other souvenirs of her past, fond memories of treasures.

Heavy, wet snow clogged the streets, and Elaine arrived much later than she'd planned. Skirting the arena, she noticed that players were already on the ice and waiting for the Monday morning team meeting. Skating would be out until after practice; her workday was about to begin.

After stashing her equipment, Elaine grabbed a clipboard and the few messages off her desk and joined the team to await Cap's entrance. The moment she walked into the rink area, she remembered again what Meg had told her about the team and the scuttle being circulated by Vosienne. Her heart skipped a beat, and she stopped at a distant bench. Pretending to retie her shoe, Elaine steadied her nerves. There was little she could do but to act as if nothing were wrong or different. After all, Roland was now removed from her life, and that, too, would soon be circulated through the grapevine.

With a deep breath she squared her shoulders and joined the players.

It went well, much the way it always did, and she was genuinely relieved to have faced them all and to have at least that much behind her. Only Vosienne seemed distant, but she discounted him altogether.

"We're in for it this morning." Phil Walters clued her in, as he joined the group. "Cap is as mad as I've ever seen him. Saturday's game was the pits, and he's hellbent."

Suddenly she wished she'd paid closer attention to the action. It was just one more item on her own personal agenda to be corrected. All Elaine remembered was the score and that there hadn't been any serious injuries.

"What does he expect from almost a whole team of rookies?" She spoke to Phil more from habit than observation.

"Perfection. What else?"

Before they could continue, Cap Holloway marched in. Cigar planted in his mouth and eyes tightly drawn into angry beads, he looked like a rotund general ready to mount a charge. Meggan and Pantier were a few paces behind him, both looking rather dismal.

"All right, listen up!" Cap began talking before he'd even reached the group. "I'm sure you are all well aware of what happened here Saturday night. But I'm here to tell you that I don't ever want to see that kind of slapstick hockey again. If it hadn't been for Roland and a few others, Salt Lake would have shut us out for sure!"

He gnawed at his cigar and paced among the team and staff. Elaine realized that his dramatics were more for the benefit of the rookies than from unmet expectations. She looked at Phil Walters; he made a shallow grin and winked. *Thank God*, she thought. Even Phil's comment had been designed to be overheard, giving Cap's act believability. She wondered, however, if Meg and Roland were just adding to the scene or if something had transpired between them.

She refused to give in to paranoia and turned back to listen to Cap's powerful rhetoric.

The coach fussed and fumed for half an hour, giving credit where credit was due and giving the rest of the team a colorful berating. When he ran out of steam, he removed the withered cigar from his mouth and gestured at Elaine.

"Doc!" He cued Elaine to stand up. "Give 'em hell if you have to," he ordered her as he started to walk out. "And I want to see you in my office after your session is over!"

Elaine flinched. His last comment was completely out of context, and she wasn't pleased to receive it. Still, she recovered and went to work.

154

"You wanted to see me?" Elaine said when she walked into Holloway's office after her power skating session had ended.

"Sure, Elaine. Close the door, won't you?" His wanting the door closed only added to her suspicions. "Pull up a chair. We need to talk."

She obeyed. There was a distance between them that she'd never sensed before, and it nearly paralyzed her. Afraid that Cap could read her mind, Elaine tried not to let her guilt and remorse surface.

"You know, Elaine, I don't like to meddle in other people's lives," he said, perched on the corner of his desk, looking down at her in front of him. "But have you given much thought to your future? Your career, that is?"

Elaine was glad to be sitting down. Her legs began to twitch nervously, and her pulse started to race. Her eyes traveled to the floor; she just couldn't look at him.

"Of course, Cap. Why do you ask?" Her voice wouldn't come forth as calmly as she wanted it to, but there was no way of retrieving the words.

"Well, now, don't get me wrong," he said as he lit another cigar. "But it seems to me that a talented woman like yourself would be wanting to consider a variety of career options. Being a trainer with a second-string hockey team isn't something to stay with a lifetime. Hardly dents your abilities, if you know what I mean. Why, I'll bet you could find a blue million other jobs that paid better and had a hell of a lot more prestige than this."

"Maybe," she said quietly. "But this is what I want to do."

"Do you really? Or are you just comfortable with it? Challenge is good for a person. Do you really think you're getting enough challenge with the Hawks?"

If he was trying to tell her she was finished, she decided to make it easy for him. "Does this mean you're not going to renew my contract for next season?" she asked with thinly disguised anger. Elaine was momentarily convinced that Holloway was working up to firing her gracefully, and she was in no mood for his locker-room diplomacy.

"Hell, no." He chuckled. "Is that what you thought?" His smile was a relief, and she tried not to sound defensive in reply.

"What else could you be leading up to?"

Cap slapped her shoulder and laughed again. "I'm talking about that offer from Dr. Caswell at the Sports Medicine Center in Indianapolis, lady." Elaine felt her entire body ease back down into the chair as he continued. "Caswell called me at home yesterday. Said he'd been trying to offer you a position there, heading up physical therapies. Said you wouldn't even go down there and look the facilities over. He really wants you for that job, Elaine. Why haven't you looked into it?"

"Because I'm perfectly happy here, Cap. Besides, what would you do for a trainer, huh?" That wasn't the complete reason, but in her current state of mind the answer was the best she could manage. Although she appreciated Holloway's interest, her rattled emotions made it hard for her to sustain a lengthy dialogue. He'd have to carry the conversation until she could regain her balance.

"I'd hire another young trainer. Don't you remember how I got you? They're out there. The Hawks could find a replacement. Think you can't be replaced, old button?" He laughed and slapped her shoulder again; it was plain, even to Cap, that his initial approach had alarmed her. "Seriously, Elaine"—and his voice grew mellow—"it's a very good opportunity, and I'm ordering you to look into it. For your own good. I'd miss you—we all would—but you're not getting any younger, y'know." He winked. "Jobs like the one in Indianapolis are rare as hens' teeth."

She could speak again; the trembling had subsided. "Thanks, Cap. And I know that you're right. It's just that I like working with younger athletes—seeing them progress along and finally become real pros. I don't know if I would like being closed up in some ivory tower of medical research. I want to work with people out in the real world."

"Then you'd better talk to Caswell. You have the whole concept wrong, Elaine. According to him, you'll work directly with amateurs in their everyday setting: schools, colleges, that sort of thing. Personally I think you can make a greater contribution to professional sports by working with kids. That's the real starting point, don't y'think?"

He stood, walked to the door, and opened it for her. Their conference was over.

"Tell me you'll think it over. I want you to do something good for Elaine for a change." His hand patted her shoulder as she started out of the office.

"I will," she said with a real smile this time. "Just for you, Cap."

"No, no," he said reprimandingly. "For *you.*"

## CHAPTER NINE

Elaine returned to her office and spent the rest of the morning in solitude, trying to recover from the emotional yo-yo that she'd been on for the past week. No one disturbed her, and the silent office became a quiet retreat in the midst of her personal turmoil.

Holloway, her own guilt and anger, Pantier, thoughts of another job—it was just too much to sort out all at once. What had happened to that well-organized, rewarding life she'd built? Whatever it was, she had lost sight of it that Monday morning.

If she had had to describe her mental state, the only applicable word would have been "confused."

*I've run through rapture, anger, disillusionment,* she thought. Of all of them, she had to admit that she preferred confusion. It was the only mental state that didn't set her adrenaline pumping and her head spinning.

Something was happening. She laughed at the absurdity of the realization. Something was happening. Her ability to reduce monumental problems to a single, asinine observation had her laughing out loud.

"At least I'm laughing," she said aloud.

"So I see" came Roland's reply. He stood in the doorway, staring at her with a whimsical expression that she couldn't interpret at once. "May I come in, or is this a private conversation?"

His comment only made her laugh harder. It felt good to

release the anxiety through something other than tears for a change. Besides, she was really glad to see him and to have him acting so naturally, as if nothing had happened.

"No, no, it's not private." She chuckled. "But if you come in, close the door. I'm not ready for group therapy yet."

He came in and closed the door behind him, then hopped up on the examining table. Nothing had *really* changed, she thought. Just looking at him still made her hot all over. But, then, something had changed. She saw how easy it would be to start it all over, just where they'd ended a few days before. No. Her mind shifted gears, and Elaine tried to temper her refound humor with common sense and restraint.

"Did you have an appointment?" she asked, remaining calm but friendly.

"Not that I know of. I've been sent here with instructions from our fearless leader, Coach Holloway." His black eyes danced with mischief.

She wanted to rush into his arms and ask him to love her right there, right then. How she ached to feel his body again, but she couldn't let him know. Not now. Even though she needed him so much now—more than ever—it couldn't be. He would only start the emotional roller coaster ride again, and she wasn't strong enough to face another turn at it.

"And what does our fearless leader have to say?" she asked.

"We're about to change the travel schedule again, I'm afraid," Pantier replied. He swung his legs carelessly over the edge of the table, looking very much like a schoolboy about to deliver a recitation. "The trip to Indianapolis next week is to be extended two extra days."

"Why?" Elaine sputtered. Had Holloway wanted her to go to Indianapolis *that* badly?

"He just got a call from the Checkers' office there. I guess we're going to play them for three games instead of two.

159

They asked Cap to split a charity game with them, and he said okay." Roland frowned as Elaine's face reflected an odd expression of confusion mixed with contempt. "What's the matter?" he asked. "Is there a problem with that?"

"I guess not" was her reply, but it was hard to shake off the obvious reason for Cap's acceptance of a charity game. In those two extra days he would expect her to check out the sports medicine offer. Now he was maneuvering her into position. It was just one more disturbing fact she'd have to face.

"You'll like that city," Roland said. "Maybe you could take a look at the Sports Medicine Center there."

"Oh, no, not you, too! What is this anyway?" she cried. "Maybe I just ought to pack up right now and take a bus!" Exasperated, she sat down at her desk and began to sort through files, ignoring him.

"Cap told me what he said to you," she heard Roland say in a serious voice. "He's right, you know. It *would* be a terrific job for you, Elaine."

"I just wish everyone would let me live my own life!" she growled. "This whole place has gone crazy." Turning toward him, she saw that he'd walked to the desk and was standing next to her. "So, if you're through, I'd like to get back to work."

"Just one more thing," he answered. Bending down to be at eye level with her, he balanced his body against her desk. "It's about Saturday night . . ."

Elaine just closed her eyes, as if she could make him disappear by merely wishing it. But before she could charm him away, Roland put his hand on her arm and kissed her on the forehead. His lips were cool against her face; she opened her eyes to find him only inches away. With his other hand Roland slowly stroked her cheek; his eyes caught hers. She knew he was hoping she'd reconsider, forgive him, start anew. Elaine saw that he was being sincere with her, but she'd made up her mind. She felt his

160

breath breeze across her neck, and the sensation made her mind swim. With all that had happened she still wanted him—desperately.

"I owe you an apology, Elaine. I'm afraid I was thoroughly insensitive. I should have realized the problems—"

"Please, Roland, don't," she whispered. "We both rushed into this. We'll share all the blame together."

"You had every right to be angry at me, you know. That little scene with Brouillion. And what I said about—"

She put her fingers to his lips and smiled. "We both said some very foolish things that night. Let's not repeat them now. It's over."

"I don't want it to be over," he answered brusquely, knowing she meant that more than their argument was finished.

"It *has* to be. If for no other reason than I can't live with this game that we've created . . . and the pressures—"

"If you mean Vosienne, I've adjusted his attitude on that score!"

"Listen to me just this once," she whispered again and ran her hand along his cheek. "We have different priorities in life, different philosophies—whatever you want to call it. I'm not prepared to change and live by your rules. I just can't justify it in my mind. Can you understand that?"

"Yes," he admitted quietly. Their eyes met for one long, loving moment. Then he stood up. Her hand fell away from his face with graceless finality.

"You mean so much to me, Elaine. Do you know," he added quickly, "that you're the first woman who's ever made me that angry? Funny, eh? You are so very special in so many ways. I know that you care for me." He slowly paced between the desk and the examining table.

"Thank you," she heard herself say. But her voice sounded lifeless, and she wondered why her words didn't come out the way she wanted them to anymore. Nothing she said seemed to sound right. Where had her conviction gone?

Pantier paced back to the desk, and Elaine stood. His hands reached out to touch her shoulders.

"I don't want you to be angry. Not at me. Not at yourself. But more . . ." He hesitated and squeezed her arms for emphasis. "But most of all, I don't want to lose what we have." His eyes looked glazed as he looked down at her. "You've made my life the best it's ever been at a time when it was the worst I've ever known. You mean so much to me, Elaine. What we have is . . ." It might have been that the English word temporarily escaped him, but for whatever reason he couldn't finish.

"It's a memory—no more, no less." Elaine inserted the words that *she* wanted him to hear.

"No," he said argumentatively, "it's more than that. You can't just call it off like that!"

"But we have to," she said, finding her courage at last. "We have to because that's all it can be for me."

He let go of her then and stood thinking. She could see his mind working through the fixed, translucent gleam in his eyes. He frowned.

"If that's how it must be for you, then I have to agree. I won't have us enemies, Elaine."

"No, not enemies," she said. Her heart felt as if it were breaking, but she refused to reconcile it any other way. Remarkably she began to sense a calm within.

He walked slowly to the door and almost turned back to face her again. He hesitated at the doorway for a long, silent moment, then lowered his head and disappeared into the hall.

Elaine locked the door behind him and cried. Her relief was forged with grief, an unnatural hybrid of emotions that temporarily delivered her from abject despair.

162

"Hustle, hustle, hustle! Go right for him, Hadly. Don't let him buffalo you. Go! Now pass to Vosienne. Grab it, Claude. That's it. Pass off to Rutledge. Rush it! Rush it! Shoot!" A whistle sounded. Everyone stopped and looked at Pantier. There was silence. Then his voice boomed out again.

"When I say shoot, I mean go for the net. Who taught you guys to shoot anyway? When you're being guarded too close to maneuver, pass the puck or skate over the guard. Those are the choices. And let me tell you, if you skate over him once, he won't get so close the next time."

They all moved to center ice, ready for another face-off. Elaine watched them work out from high above the arena. Each practice session for weeks had found her perched in the press box, watching and listening to Pantier's demanding instruction. She was on hand in case of injury, but Elaine knew that she was really there to watch Roland. It was a way to be near him without drawing any undue attention. She doubted if he even saw her, and that was the way she wanted it.

Time was nearly up; each day that they both remained in Omaha was precious to her. In less than a week now Pantier was scheduled to leave for Edmonton; shortly after that she would probably be gone, too.

Knees tucked beneath her chin, Elaine sat with her arms around her legs, hidden from view and thinking about the past. Since Thanksgiving the roller coaster ride had gotten worse. On the pain of losing Roland, she'd superimposed a decision to leave the Hawks as well.

It amazed her how quickly the break had happened; still, she realized that the decision hadn't been made without days of agonizing introspection. Before she even visited Dr. Caswell at the Sports Medicine Center, Elaine had decided to take his job offer.

But now, every day, when she viewed the players working out together, Elaine wondered if she could ever forget having had the Hawks and Pantier in her life. Realistically she knew that no matter where she went or what field she worked in, her memories would haunt her. Pantier, in particular, would remain vivid in her mind. And it was that one simple fact that motivated her to leave Omaha—and her past—behind.

During the days since their breakup she had vacillated between the normal routine of work and training, moving in nearly normal pace to the hum of activity and excitement of the arena. At night, though, her imagination lived for those blissful weeks when they had been one.

Watching him play during the games only added to her memory's bank. When Pantier left the team, Elaine feared she would still see him, there on the ice, like a mirage that taunted her, always summoning her back into the past.

She wrestled with another dragon of her mind for the two weeks before the team went to Indianapolis. Having conquered the fear of risking, Elaine was vexed by a vague sense of not having overcome anything at all. Something still stirred within her, making her days a heavy burden and her nights a living hell.

Only on the day before they went on the road was she able to focus on the real problem. She feared the future, a future full of painful memories. What had seemed pleasant years of meaningful work and strong ties had become a hodgepodge of personal suffering.

The happy, rewarding times had been overshadowed, and as she grieved for Roland's love, Elaine saw more clearly how little she'd really accomplished. Optimism abandoned her. She relinquished it to cold reality. The past must be firmly separated from the future.

Remembering Cap's words, Elaine forced herself to make decisions, for her own sake. If she wanted to start fresh and find peace of mind, she must make an attempt to rebuild her life in another place with another career. Omaha and hockey must be left behind.

Perhaps Roland had been right when he said she couldn't go on living in the past. His viewpoint made her question every reason she'd ever had for staying with the Hawks. In the end she saw that her own shattered dreams, one by one, had been lived out through the team.

Her career plans as a skater had been destroyed, so she had lived out her dreams through the young players who skated *for* her. Elaine even wondered if her marriage to Tony had been just another means of escaping reality. And when he was gone, she had become even more withdrawn.

Elaine was very hard on herself as she purged her mind and fought the dragon of the future. By the time she reached Dr. Caswell's office, Elaine saw his job offer as a lifesaver. Her future depended on it. As if the position were a rope tossed to a drowning man, she grasped it and vowed not to let go. It seemed like a small sacrifice to make when her very existence was threatened. She was being offered a place to run to, some shelter from the past, and a way into tomorrow. Fate, she thought, had handed her an option.

"Elaine, I'm so glad to see you again!" Dr. Caswell greeted her as she walked into the suite of offices that served as the center's temporary headquarters. "It's been quite a few years, but you haven't changed a bit."

She smiled and took the seat he offered. Amol Caswell hadn't really changed much either; he didn't look his sixty-plus years, although she suspected his waistline had increased some. Yet the balding, cherub-faced doctor was just as she remembered him from her college days.

Thoughtful, exuberant, and kindly, Caswell was a leading orthopedic specialist, who knew what he wanted and how to get it. His ability to organize and promote, along with his medical credentials, had virtually guaranteed the success of any project he supported.

The Sports Medicine Center was a personal dream, and

in only five years Caswell had brought it to actuality through almost single-handed effort.

"This is all temporary, my dear," he told Elaine, indicating the sparsely equipped offices. "Our building will be completed in another month, and we'll be much more organized and comfortable."

For the interim the center worked within the therapy and laboratory facilities of Indiana University's medical complex.

"But very soon now," he assured her, "we'll have all but major surgery housed in our own facility."

Caswell showed her the detailed plans for the center, and on their way to lunch he even drove her to the construction site. As promised, it was going to be a magnificent monument to sports research and to Dr. Caswell's driving spirit.

Elaine found herself infected with his enthusiasm, and the afternoon was spent in discussing the center's ideology in general and what Caswell anticipated for physical therapy in particular.

They easily shared personal ideas and proposed methods. As the day was ending, Elaine felt much better about the job, even though her suspicions had been confirmed. She didn't relish the laboratory work, but having an opportunity to work with Caswell again made the offer palatable.

"So, Elaine, what do you think?" he asked late in the afternoon. "Would you like to join us?"

They'd already discussed salary and responsibilities. The salary was generous; the responsibilities bordered on repetitive and cloistered.

"I'm very impressed with your objectives, Doctor," she replied. "But I was hoping for more education-oriented involvement with the athletes." Truthfully she was disappointed with the antiseptic approach.

"Well, that will come in time," he answered. "First, we must discover what athletes need; then we can educate

166

them. I'm sure you're used to more spontaneous methods, but we're here to do research. It takes a more structured approach."

Elaine accepted the job, as she had known she would, without any further argument. Only one requirement caused her to hesitate.

"I know this is asking a lot, Elaine," he explained after her acceptance. "But we need you here and functioning by mid-January. Do you think you can arrange for a replacement in Omaha by, say, January twentieth?"

She'd already made the mistake of telling Caswell that the team could pull a temporary trainer from the league pool if necessary. Now she had no alternative but to go along with him.

Caswell assured her he would find her housing at the medical school while she relocated, but it still meant putting the condo up for sale immediately, shuffling her possessions in and out of storage and an amalgamation of hundreds of other details over the next month. Still, she accepted the situation, thinking it the only practical alternative.

As the Hawks struggled through their three-game bill at Indianapolis, Elaine retreated into thought once more. Oblivious to the games, the after-hours celebrating, even to Meggan's constant companionship, she began planning her move.

Until the team was homeward bound, Elaine found comfort in her thoughts. Having something concrete demanding her attention was a mixed blessing. There was no time to reflect on Roland and the past; she chose to observe the activity around her rather than to participate. It relieved the painful reality of separation, at least for a few days.

"How about dinner at Murphy's when we get back?" Meg cornered her as they flew back to Omaha. "It'll be too late to cook at home."

167

Elaine had to chuckle. "What time is too late to cook at home?" she asked.

"Just about anytime after five A.M. for me. How about it? We haven't had a quiet meal alone in weeks." Meg had grown concerned over Elaine's withdrawn state. Since the breakup with Roland, Elaine had been silent and spiritless, but only Meg knew how seriously withdrawn her friend had become.

While Roland still attempted to be friendly, Elaine held him at a distance. They spoke, but never alone. She refused his invitations to dinner, and just in case he tried to join her table, Elaine always made it a point to sit with the coaching staff or a half dozen players.

Their relationship was peaceful—a truce at best—but Meg felt her friend's sorrow keenly.

"On for dinner?" Elaine hadn't answered her yet, and Meg was not going to take her silent refusal.

"Okay," Elaine replied. She glanced over at Meg and smiled. Suddenly she realized how little time she had left with Meg, Cap, and the others. "But it's my treat." Of all her treasures, Meg Holloway's friendship was the most priceless to her.

The flight home brought Elaine back to the present. She'd spent nearly three weeks either reliving the past or visualizing the future; the present was slipping away.

The team was high after its three unprecedented victories over the Indianapolis Checkers. The players roamed the plane's aisle, talked to the stewardesses, and entertained the other passengers with good-natured jokes and conversation. Elaine had almost forgotten how good it felt to be with them, and the thought of leaving stung her sharply.

She had to go, she reminded herself. But for the rest of her time with them she wanted to be a part of all the good things her life with hockey had meant.

"Did I tell you that I'm going home for Christmas?" she

said to Meggan as they ate later at Murphy's. The team was all there, and they had to shout over the noise.

"Home?" Meg echoed. "No. When did you decide that?" Elaine's declaration disturbed her; she usually returned to Boston for one month in the summer and celebrated the holidays with Meg.

"Oh, I just decided it would be a good idea for a change." What Elaine didn't say was that she *had* to take the time for a visit with her family before starting the job at Indianapolis. She wouldn't be eligible for vacation time her first year with the center.

"When will you be leaving?" Meg pushed for the information. The Hawks would play their last game before Christmas on Wednesday, and the holiday fell on Saturday. That meant Meggan had only five days, at the very most, before Elaine left.

"I plan to fly out Friday afternoon." Her real plan was to pull a few strings with the team's travel agent to get a round-trip ticket on short notice.

Meg was silent. Her mind raced at supersonic speed. She didn't like the uneasy sensation that Elaine's plans gave her.

"May I join you ladies?" Roland interrupted. "Or is this a private celebration?"

"Not at all," said Elaine. "Join us." It was safe enough, she thought. Knowing how he still affected her, Elaine didn't feel that she could trust herself to be alone with Pantier. But she enjoyed having him near, even if he constantly tried to mend the breach between them.

"I see Joe over there," said Meg, standing and moving away from the table. "I'll be back in a minute. I have to talk to him."

Roland and Elaine were alone for the first time in weeks, and Elaine wanted to call Meg back; Meg was a good buffer between her and Roland. Panic was rising inside her. *Calm, be calm,* she said to herself and took a deep breath.

169

"I wanted to hear about your tour of the Sports Medicine Center," Roland asked. "Wish I could have joined you. What was it like?"

Elaine decided to give her meeting with Caswell more punch than it deserved. If for no other reason than to make Roland believe she was firm in her conviction, she wanted him to see her as poised and unemotional at that moment, even though her heart pounded with anxiety. Elaine was cutting ties with the past, removing Meg, the Hawks, everything she cared about from her life. And that pain, combined with the trauma of losing Pantier, was almost unbearable.

Roland, Meg, everyone must believe that she wanted the job in Indianapolis.

"It's a very impressive position," she explained to Pantier, trying to act at ease. "I'd forgotten how wonderful Dr. Caswell is. We worked together when I was in college, you know." Yes, he remembered her telling him that.

"So what did you decide?" He wasn't sidestepping the issue. Curiosity was one of Roland's strong points.

"I'm still thinking it over. Is that okay?" Elaine wouldn't have Pantier knowing her plans before she'd had an opportunity to tell Cap in person.

"Good." Her answer seemed to please him. "Probably too many test tubes for you anyway." Dropping the subject there, they switched to talking about the completed games at Indianapolis and the real progress made by the team since Thanksgiving.

Elaine relaxed a little and let the conversation flow. This was how she wanted to remember him.

Pantier offered her a ride home, and she accepted. Nothing in his actions told her that he expected more, and, true to his word, Roland took her straight to her front door.

"Thank you for another lovely evening, Panther-person." Elaine chuckled as they stood on the threshold of her front door. Perhaps it was having made a decision that gave

170

her renewed confidence with him. Whatever it was, she felt their old rapport again.

"Oh, no," he retorted. "Thank *you*." Before she could stop him, Roland swept her into his arms and kissed her. Elaine considered fighting him but didn't. His body overpowered her. His scent, the warmth of his arms, the cool shimmer of his lips as they met her mouth—everything about him aroused her anew. They had been apart for weeks, and she had ached for him each and every minute of every day. Had he but offered, she would have surrendered to any demand he made right then. She wanted him more than life. If only he loved her, Elaine would have followed him anywhere.

"I miss you so, my little Work of Art," he whispered. "Can't you see how much I need you, Elaine?" His fingers brushed along her cheekbone and sent waves of intense voltage surging through her frame.

Her eyes filled with tears. Everything she'd ever known was coming to an end, and she was numb with grief. "And I miss you, Roland." She stopped short of telling him how much she needed him, too. "Honestly, I miss you, but it's not meant to be. Can't you understand that?"

He smiled wistfully at her, then gave her another kiss. "I understand why," he replied, "and I respect you for it, Elaine. But I refuse to accept it. Good night." Roland turned and walked back to his car.


Nestled high on her perch near the press box, Elaine thought back on it all. The taste of his mouth still lingered on her lips from the night before.

Below her the team practiced for its match with Milwaukee the next night, but Elaine concentrated on Pantier. His fluid movements, the powerful thrust of his legs, and the determination of his voice reminded her to be honest with herself.

Yes, she loved him. She loved him so much that it hurt.

But she also loved him enough to let him go—to let him be what he was and to do what he needed to do.

Elaine only hoped that someday he would understand why she would not change her mind. Just like Roland, she had a right to be herself, to demand what she needed without apology.

She needed to be loved for a lifetime, just as Roland needed to be free.

# CHAPTER TEN

Elaine made a point of stopping by Cap's office before she left that night. She had to tell him about accepting the job at Indianapolis. As much as she wanted to wait, to put it off until after Christmas, it wasn't fair to him or the Hawks.

*It's just another ending of the past,* she told herself. Besides, knowing that Cap had virtually ordered her to check into Caswell's offer made her more confident of his reaction.

"Do you have a minute?" she asked the coach as she stood in the doorway to his office.

"For you I always have time. Pull up a chair, Elaine." He handed her a stick of gum, and she sat down.

"What's up?"

"Well," she began hesitantly, "I wanted to report back to you on my meeting with Dr. Caswell in Indianapolis."

Cap looked blank for a second, then frowned. "Oh, yeah," he stammered. "I forgot about that."

He'd forgotten about it? Elaine barely comprehended his statement. How could he have forgotten a direct order like that?

"I made an appointment and spent the whole day with him at the center," she said, hoping to jog his memory and feeling strange about his reaction.

"Good. Good. What did you think of it?" Cap regained his equilibrium and tried to navigate back into the conversation.

"They have some wonderful plans, their permanent building is almost completed, and it was nice to talk with Dr. Caswell again."

"That's nice," he replied, looking confused again. "Is that what you wanted to tell me?"

"Well, no." His attitude threw Elaine completely off-balance. "I came in to tell you that I've accepted the offer."

Cap stopped wobbling in his swivel chair and looked at her. Elaine didn't know what else to add, so she just looked at him and waited.

"I see. Yes." The coach stood up and began pacing the small space behind his desk. "Then they expect you to report in April." He wasn't asking her; he assumed her new job would begin at the end of the hockey season.

"Actually"—Elaine took a deep breath—"they need me to start right away. I'm to report by January twentieth." From her previous conversation with Holloway, Elaine had been sure that her contract could be waived if she took the Sports Medicine Center position. And it had never occurred to her to mention any contract problems to Caswell. Now, with Cap's sudden loss of memory, she didn't know what to do or say.

"If it's my contract," she began again, "I'll guarantee a replacement myself."

"That won't be a problem, Elaine." Cap returned to his chair and plopped down in it. "I'm really pleased for you if it's what you want." His voice was somber; his eyes were tiny lights beneath a furrowed brow. "Why don't we talk more about it later? I'd like to digest this for a day or two and then get back with you."

She left his office that afternoon not knowing how to react. Obviously he wasn't pleased that she'd followed his advice. And that wasn't like Cap: He never forgot a word he said, and he did not renege on agreements. His reaction had been odd.

By game time that night Elaine was too busy to give

174

Cap's strange reaction much more thought. She hurried through her pregame ritual in her office and was checking her med kit when the door squeaked open behind her. Turning, she saw Pantier enter.

"Yes?"

"I wanted to see if you were going over to Murphy's after the game."

The Hawks were having their communal Christmas party that night after the game. Meggan had already reminded Elaine earlier that day.

"I was planning on it," Elaine replied evenly. Thankful that Pantier did not come any closer to her, she watched him from across the room, while he smiled at her with bright, mischievous eyes.

He looked younger than his years somehow; he reminded her of an aspiring rookie, enjoying the surprises of a world untested—a yong man at the beginning of his career, just starting his life. Perhaps, if they had met then, when the world was fresh and inviting, it wouldn't have ended like this. Maybe their love could have grown and become more important than career standings and professional reputations. Maybe . . . Elaine forced herself to stop the wishful thinking right there. It was simply too late for them.

"I was hoping to get a ride if you don't mind," Pantier finally said to her. "I really need to talk with you, Elaine, and I thought we might ride over to the restaurant together . . . give us a few minutes alone to talk."

"Please, Roland," Elaine struggled to say. "Please, don't. . . ."

"It's Christmas, Elaine. Give me a break." Pantier continued to smile, seemingly unperturbed by her objections. "I've got some great news to tell you, and I don't want anyone else knowing it before you do."

The final buzzer sounded, and she conceded. "All right. I'll meet you outside the dressing room after the game."

"If I'm not out in fifteen minutes, would you come in and get me?" he asked with a smirk, turning to leave.

"No!" She laughed. "Now get out of here!" He left and barely avoided the towel she threw after him. He was impossible, she thought. Beautiful, full of life, and impossible. And her heart was breaking at the thought of never seeing him again. Her laughter ended in a sob.

From the first face-off the game was electrified. It was Roland's last game with the Hawks, and everyone could see that the team meant to chalk up a dynamic victory as his going-away gift from Omaha. But Pantier must have decided on the same gift to show his appreciation, and the coach was cooperating with him. During the first period the Panther was in every other line change, and he skated harder and faster than he ever had.

It wasn't possible to go on automatic pilot that night. She watched his every move, shouted her lungs out for his effort, and indulged the wildly electric sensation that his power and grace caused.

With less than a minute to go in the first period, Roland was squaring up for another goal drive. The crowd was on their feet. The arena organist was pumping out a throbbing chord to heighten the tension, and Elaine held her breath as he stormed across the center blue line.

A Milwaukee guard, twice Pantier's size, skated inches away from him, refusing to give way to Roland's determined shot. True to his theory, Roland passed off to Hadly. The Milwaukee player started to veer off in pursuit, but he was a second too slow. As he shifted to follow Hadly, his stick caught Roland behind the knee. Both players went down without warning. Neither was able to brace his fall, and Roland lay on the ice, beneath the much larger player.

Elaine was on the ice and moving toward them before play was even stopped. Several players helped roll the Milwaukee man off Roland. Elaine ordered him to stay down on the ice until their trainer checked him out, and she bent over Pantier, who lay doubled up in pain.

"My ankle. It's my ankle," he kept moaning.

"Lie on your back," she ordered sternly. He did as she requested, and Elaine carefully cut off his sock and removed what was left of his shin guard. Upon impact, the protecting shin gear had impaled Roland's ankle. "Stretcher!" she shouted back over her shoulder.

"Is it?"

"Lie still. I can't tell. We've got to get you X-rayed."

"Oh, God, no, no . . ." His voice crackled with pain and fear. He knew the ankle was broken; she didn't have to tell him.


The hospital emergency room was deathly quiet that evening as Meg and Elaine waited for the surgeon. Shortly after eleven Cap and Phil came in.

"How is he?" Cap wanted to know.

"He's in surgery. We haven't seen the doctor yet."

"Bad?"

"Yes, the surgeon thought so," Elaine replied.

Moments later the surgeon came out to tell them that Pantier had sustained a complicated ankle break and several torn muscles. "He's not going to do any more power skating. That ankle has taken all it can, I'm afraid. We did the best we could, but . . ."

They all understood. Cap thanked the doctor, and Elaine asked when he would be out of recovery.

"Not until morning. Come back anytime after eight, and you can see him then."


Elaine went home but never slept. By eight the next morning she had located Roland's private room. She entered to find him propped up in bed, his leg in a cast. He didn't look up as she walked over to the bed.

177

"Did you rest well?" She couldn't think of anything more comforting to say. He looked sullen and withdrawn.

"Yeah, I got a lot of rest," he said with a sneer. "You sleep really well after surgery." Still, he did not look at her.

Seeing him there, helpless and dejected, brought tears to her eyes, but she forced them down. He mustn't see how deeply she felt his pain. No, now he really needed all the strength she could give him.

"Are they giving you anything for the pain?" she asked, and he looked up and glared at her silently. "Can I get you anything?"

"Yeah—two legs, ten years younger than these," he finally answered in a strained voice.

"I know how you must feel . . ." she began to say.

"Do you? Really?" he snarled. His eyes snapped at her, and she momentarily froze in his gaze. "Don't be kind, Elaine. I don't need sympathy. Especially from someone who has *no* idea how I really feel right now."

He looked away from her and concentrated on some unseen point in space above the bed.

His words were to be expected. She'd heard them before. Yet, coming from Pantier, she read more into his meaning. It was not like him to take defeat and wallow in his own misery. His will seemed gone; his eyes were vacant, and she saw signs of self-pity and resignation in his face. His professional playing career was over.

The great black Panther would have to face life on different terms now. And she loved him enough to do what had to be done—for his sake. Elaine squared her shoulders and took a deep breath.

"Do you think you have some corner on the injury market?" she said to him slowly. "What do you want, Roland? Wasn't eighteen years of professional hockey enough, or were you naïve enough to believe that it would go on forever?"

Again his eyes met hers; there was no reply.

"And you think I can't understand how you feel right now. You must think you're the only athlete who ever faced the end of a career." Her anger rose as he stared beyond her. "Look at me when I'm talking to you, Roland!" He still looked away. "You've had a career that most of us only dream of. And now that it's over, you think you deserve more?"

Pantier lay motionless, facing the wall, but she continued all the same.

"Fourteen years ago—that's when my career ended. You think I don't know how you feel? Well, let me tell you a thing or two." Slowly he turned to face her. "I've skated all my life. I practiced when other children were having birthday parties and going to the movies. I competed at every event my family could afford to enter me in. And I worked at it, all the time knowing I could make the Olympics if I just worked hard and long enough. I lived to compete. Just like you."

Her eyes, clear and intense, held his. Her body straightened, and her chin rose in defiance as she continued.

"And I made the team, because I worked for it. Competition, perfection—they were my only goals." Never flinching or shifting, she let the silence between them punctuate her argument. "One month before the games I fell and broke my hip. And the only damn thing I could think of was getting well and spending four more years training for the next games. So I went for it. Four years later I had to face the truth when I couldn't even make the second round of preliminaries."

Though his expression remained unchanged, Pantier's eyes closed suddenly.

"I learned a great deal about myself and my goals after that, and I decided that skating was my life. Competition and perfection were secondary. I took up physical therapy and sports med, and eight years ago I signed with the

Hawks because I thought I could use my knowledge and skills to help others reach their potential."

Somehow the anger had evaporated during her speech; the last few sentences were merely factual, not hostile. The emotions, however, that memory had dredged up had depleted her physically, and Elaine sat down on the edge of his bed.

"You've had a wonderful career, Roland, many more years than most. And I believe you can still use all you've learned. You can keep on giving, as you call it, just in a different way." She pushed herself up to leave. "The past is past; tomorrow is what you make it. Don't drop out of life just when you have the most to give. Don't be selfish. A lot of people can use what you have to offer."

His eyes opened. Wide black eyes glistened with moisture, and he nodded his head ever so slightly before closing his eyes again and sinking into the soft pillow.

Silently she left the room and went home to pack.

The weather took a decided turn for the worse that night. The barometer was bottoming out; the temperature dropped rapidly. It snowed all night. The next morning, packed and anxious now to leave, Elaine listened to the morning forecast on WOW and prayed it wasn't true.

She stood at the kitchen window, concentrating on the broadcaster's gloomy outlook. The narrow span of ground between her home and the woods lay hidden under nine inches of new-fallen snow, and the sky was heavy with the promise of more.

Damp, clumped flakes fell against the window glass; the woods beyond were barely visible behind the icy curtain of silent, heavy snow. The scene was quiet now, but if the forecast of gusty winds and sub-zero temperatures came to pass . . . She shivered. Omaha was preparing for a full-scale blizzard.

The kitchen phone jangled. Elaine jumped to answer it, hoping it was Roland. Instead, it was Meggan.

"Have you heard the forecast?" Meg gasped.

"Just now," Elaine answered. "I was thinking about calling the airport about my flight. I'm due to leave at four forty."

"It doesn't sound too good," Meg replied. "This storm's supposed to hit around noon." The airport would be closed; everything would be in suspended animation until the blizzard spent itself or moved on. "Joe is trying to buy a few things at the grocery right now. We can pool our food if it gets really bad."

Meggan wasn't overreacting, and Elaine appreciated her forethought. They both had been through storms like this before. If it got bad, they could expect to be buried for days, forced into hibernation until the wind abated and the city crews came to dig them out.

"I'll check my pantry," Elaine told her, "but I think I've got enough to carry me a week or so." She meant she had enough canned goods to live on. If power was lost, there'd be no cooking or heat.

They discussed a short list of problems to be faced, agreed to move into one condo or the other in case the power went out, and Elaine said she'd let Meg know as soon as she knew something definite about her flight to Boston. It was a routine they'd been over before. Meg had deemed it their prairie disaster plan for winter emergencies. And in Omaha winter emergencies meant blizzard.

Thankfully Meg hadn't asked about Roland. Elaine was glad for a reprieve. She hadn't stopped thinking of him since the visit of the morning before, and she certainly didn't want to discuss it with anyone.

It was impossible to get through to the airport, and after dialing a dozen or more times, Elaine gave up. Turning off WOW, she flipped on the television. There would be a constant flow of information about the storm on the local

181

channels; they would confirm the airport situation, so she waited for the news.

By eleven that morning the wind began to build. It shook the west windows, and she thought about unpacking right then. But desperate hope kept her immobile before the television. Wrapped in her unhappiness and unwilling to accept another inevitability, she sat on the sofa, absorbing every word about the approaching storm.

Around noon it occurred to her to call Roland at the hospital, but she didn't. Instead, she decided to let her mind dwell on him—to give play to the thoughts and feelings about him. He'd never left her conscious mind these past twenty-four hours. She would let him remain in her heart and mind. A phone call could never satisfy the need she felt and the frustration he was experiencing. No, Roland was safe there in the hospital: warm, well fed, and reasonably pampered. Why call him now? Everything had been said.

Still, she missed him, and the pending isolation of the storm depressed her even more. There would be no escape from her thoughts or the past.

By one o'clock, as the wind built to a steady, noisy pulse at the window, she unpacked her suitcases and resigned herself to working through the holidays alone. Perhaps this was really what she needed. Instead of running away to Boston, postponing the pain, perhaps it would be best to stay and work out all the memories in solitude right then and there.

At midafternoon she began turning on lights. It was dark; the storm blocked the dim winter sun. The wind was a steady moan outside. The house grew colder, as arctic air drew out the heat faster than the furnace could supply it.

Meg called again with the updated food report. "Joe just made it back," she babbled. "He's nearly frozen from walking."

"He didn't drive?" Elaine gasped. In thirty-mile-an-hour

wind anyone could freeze in a matter of minutes. The wind chill had hit minus thirty and was still dropping.

"Yes. But the car stalled a block away. He's okay. But it took him six hours to get back." It sounded like a normal blizzard story, Elaine thought. No one was ever ready for one, and every grocery in the city was probably mobbed with last-minute panic buyers.

Meggan's voice was comforting. Elaine was unusually lonely. The storm, Roland, her thoughts—she yearned for companionship. She longed for Roland. Still, when Meg invited her over for dinner, she declined.

"Not together, Meg. Thanks."

"Hey, it's only thirty feet to my front door," Meg argued.

"Right. Thirty feet at thirty below!" Elaine tried to laugh. But Meg persisted. Finally, Elaine said, "Maybe," and that appeased Meg.

An hour later Elaine was still listening to the evening news while she tried to fix something to eat. Her appetite was nonexistent; the news was bleak. She turned down the TV and paced back into the kitchen.

A second later, above the howling of the wind, she heard a knock at the front door. Meg no doubt. She never could take no for an answer.

Elaine bounded to the door and pulled it open carefully. Bitter cold air rushed in, a whirl of powdered snow clouded the doorway, and in the cloud stood Roland.

"Mind if I come in?" he asked cheerfully.

"Oh, my . . . yes, yes, come in," Elaine babbled. He swung through the door on crutches hidden beneath his Sherpa coat. His hair formed a black fur trim along the outer edge of his knit cap; his mustache was spiked with snow.

"Where did you come from? How did you get here?" Elaine managed to stumble through a dozen more questions as he took off his coat, hat, and gloves and handed her the crutches. "Why are you out on a night like this on crutches, you . . ."

"I happened to be in the neighborhood and wanted to make sure I didn't miss getting stranded with you." Pantier now stood before her in layered sweaters and a pair of jeans slashed to the knee because of the cast on his lower leg and foot.

"Oh, no, you don't, Roland." Elaine tried to sound determined, but again her voice didn't cooperate. "Did you injure your head, huh?" He just smiled and took back his crutches.

"Do I smell food? Dinner? I'm starving. Hospital food is lethal." With that he swung toward the kitchen, Elaine in pursuit.

"How did you get over here? You aren't supposed to be out of the hospital. What did you do, sign yourself out?"

"As a matter of fact," he said, "I did. But the really hard part was getting a cab home." Elaine pulled a chair out, he sat down, and she helped him lift the cast leg onto another chair.

"We're in the middle of a blizzard." She continued to babble. "Cabs don't run on normal schedules during a blizzard, dimwit."

"Well, if it hadn't been for Joe, I might not have made it on time," he added nonchalantly. "He picked me up this afternoon." So that was why he'd been gone to the "grocery" for six hours.

"How long have you been over at Meg's?" Elaine asked.

"About an hour. And that was long enough! Those two lovebirds are hard to be around for long. Know what I mean?" She did, but his explanation wasn't quite good enough. Roland was working very hard at appearing relaxed and self-assured. That wonderful something—the old game they used to play—was in full play once more.

"So you decided to camp out over here for the duration, eh?" Elaine stood in front of him, pointing a wooden spoon she had originally carried to the door. She was excited, buoyant. Roland was back; nothing else mattered now.

"Careful how you point that, Elaine. It could be loaded, you know."

"Well, I suggest you put yourself together and head back to the big camp-out at Meggan's," she said, not really meaning it but compelled to maintain the charade he'd begun.

"You mean to say you would turn out a poor, injured hockey player—*on crutches*—on a night like this? Back into the storm? I could freeze to death out there. A few minutes, and poof—frozen Panther!" Elaine laughed involuntarily and shook her head. He was impossible, and she was glad to see him. "Besides, as I remember, we had a date."

"That was two nights ago."

"So I'm running late. Something unexpected came up."

She offered him dinner and dismissed any further thought of evicting him.

"Don't you even want to hear my good news?" He persisted while Elaine nervously returned to the stove.

"All right, what is it?" His humor was undaunted, the easiness between them was unfailing, and Elaine felt the old electricity sparking again.

"I've been offered a terrific job."

"But you have, I mean . . ." she stammered.

"I got this offer before I busted my ankle. That's one of the things I wanted to tell you the other night. Anyway," he went on cheerfully, "there's this hockey club that's looking for a new coach. Very prestigious outfit. Of course, I'd have to relocate, but the money's good."

Elaine was genuinely pleased for him. "Oh, Roland, that's wonderful," she cried and gave him a kiss of congratulations. "Even with your injury, you can coach!"

"I'd rather be an on-ice coach," he replied, pulling her onto his lap. "But I've got time to mend. And after your rousing pep talk the other day . . ." Elaine made a face, and he laughed at her. "After that little speech I think I can handle it all okay." His hands reached to her waist, and his fingers kneaded the tight flesh beneath her sweater, making her weak again. "And as if that's not enough"—he flashed a broad smile—"this same team happens to need a trainer."

Her smiled faded, and Elaine tried to stand up, but Roland held her on his lap. "I'm sorry to disappoint you and this team, Roland, but I've accepted the job at Indianapolis. I start in January." Much to her surprise, he didn't frown.

"I know. Holloway told me. But I'm afraid you'll just have to tell Caswell you're unable to accept the job after all. This little club I'm signing with is called the Omaha Hawks, and it has some big aspirations, so it needs the best in coaches and trainers."

Elaine gasped. "You're taking Cap's place?"

"Yes, he's decided to retire, and he talked to me about taking over. We were waiting for the owners' approval; it came in on Wednesday just before game time."

When she tried to speak again, Roland simply put two fingers up to her lips and continued without further comment. "You see, Elaine, I have this philosophy—"

"Roland, please," she was able to say through his fingers.

"It's not proved yet. But I have come to believe that married athletes should never work in separate cities." He removed his hand from her mouth and grinned. Elaine was speechless. "I assume, by your silence, that you agree. That's good." He pulled her to him and kissed her hard; Elaine melted into his body. "I love you, Elaine, and I don't want to live without you."

She gazed at the velvet-eyed Panther that had captured her heart and whispered, "I love you, too. And I didn't know how I was ever going to forget you, Roland."

"Ah"—he chuckled—"I *am* so unforgettable!" He smiled and reached into his sweater. "I was going to ask you to marry me last Wednesday," he continued. "Then I experienced a minor technical difficulty." From his pocket appeared a ring box. Roland opened it and put the diamond ring on her left finger.

"Will you marry me, my Work of Art?" In complete sincerity he kissed her hand, and his black eyes pleaded for an answer.

"Oh, yes, my love," she answered through tears of joy. She wrapped her arms around his broad neck and kissed every inch of his face—from cheek to cheek. "Oh, yes, yes."

Beyond them winter pounded at the earth, but in their hearts the hope of spring and a million tomorrows was sown.

# LAURA LONDON

## Let her magical romances enchant you with their tenderness.

For glorious, romantic storytelling at its very best, get lost in these novels of 19th century London.

___ A HEART TOO PROUD ... 13498-6   $2.95

___ THE BAD BARON'S
   DAUGHTER ............................ 10735-0   2.95

___ THE GYPSY HEIRESS ......... 12960-5   2.95

# *Candlelight*

# *Ecstasy Romances*™

**$1.95 each**

At your local bookstore or use this handy coupon for ordering:

DELL BOOKS-Dept. B741D
P.O. BOX 1000, PINE BROOK, N.J. 07058-1000

Please send me the books I have checked above. I am enclosing $_____ (please add 75c per copy to
cover postage and handling). Send check or money order—no cash or C.O.D.'s. Please allow up to 8 weeks for
shipment

Name _____

Address _____

City _____ State/Zip _____